The Wind

Eric Carasella

iUniverse, Inc.
New York   Bloomington

The Wind

iUniverse books may be ordered through booksellers or by contacting:

iUniverse
1663 Liberty Drive
Bloomington, IN 47403
www.iuniverse.com
1-800-Authors (1-800-288-4677)

ISBN: 978-1-4401-2931-5 (pbk)
ISBN: 978-1-4401-2929-2 (cloth)
ISBN: 978-1-4401-2930-8 (ebk)

Printed in the United States of America

iUniverse rev. date: 3/9/2009

(1)

The house on Mercy Street had been empty for only two months. The previous owners had moved out after just two short weeks and had left the place empty and deserted. A large white For Sale sign hung in the front lawn as a reminder for the only other house on the block that its counterpart needed new ownership. A company called Research Land and Development took the property from the previous owners and used their down payment to fund a new sale. Richard LeBrock, the man responsible for selling the house and also the CEO of Research Land and Development, took extra special care in cleaning up and making new a property that was in much need of a facelift. The only other house on Mercy, a twelve room Tudor situated on eight acres of green land, had the same occupants in it for the last seven decades. The family that lived there, the Cray's, was weary of why their neighbors might be abandoning their new home after only two weeks.

Richard Lebrock took the time to visit the Crays one sunny afternoon, not long after the occupants of the only other house on Mercy bailed. He knocked on the large oak door and was greeted by the pleasant face of one Mrs. Harriet Cray. She smiled at Richard when she opened the door. The Crays were nothing if not cordial.

"I'm sorry to bother you. My name is Richard LeBrock and I am in charge of the property next door." Richard smiled at this. To say that the only other house on Mercy was next door seemed almost comical. From one front door to the other was a space of about 150 yards. The length of one and a half football fields. Richard's favorite team was the Bears.

"It's no trouble at all, Mr. LeBrock. Won't you come in," said Harriet.

Richard entered the living room of the beautiful Tudor and sat when offered a place on the couch. "I would just like to ask a few questions about the folks who were living next door for the past two weeks," Richard said.

"Have they done something wrong?" Harriet asked, sounding genuinely shocked at the very idea.

"Well, no. They simply moved out. They called me very early this morning and said that they had packed up all of their things and were loading up a van. I asked what on earth could have happened to make them want to move so suddenly. The only response I got was a click and a dead line."

"That's very strange, indeed," Harriet said.

"That is strange, no doubt. But if you could see the house now, just a few short hours after the former tenants moved out, you would be simply amazed."

"And why is that?"

"It's spotless. Not a single bit of debris left over. Not a scrap of paper, not a crumb on the kitchen counters. Nothing. It's like they were never there."

At this, Harriet Cray stood up and started pacing. She wrung her hands together like a woman who could not be more nervous. Something had rattled her cage and Richard LeBrock took note of it.

"Is something wrong, Mrs. Cray?" Richard asked.

"Well, frankly, yes. Something is very wrong."

She continued her pacing and hand wringing and only occasionally looked up at Richard LeBrock.

"Well, what is it?" Richard asked.

(2)

Anthony Morrison slid back into bed. It was only four-thirty in the morning and the house was still quiet. But he had to pee real badly. So he did his business and then slid back into bed where his wife was curled up sleeping. Anthony kissed his wife's back and snuggled up against her. He knew the kids would not be waking up for at least another three hours. He also knew that if he didn't go back to sleep he would not be in shape to handle the coming day's events. He rolled onto his back and stared at the ceiling, knowing that going back to sleep was going to be next to impossible. He had way too much on his mind.

The biggest thing was the new house. He knew his family would support any decision he made, but he also wanted them to like it as much as he did. He wanted them to fall in love at the very sight of it just like he had. But he wouldn't force the issue, either. If they decided against it, then he would bite his tongue and keep looking. After all, they were a family. He never ran his home like some horrible dictatorship. He always respected what his kids had to say, and most especially what his wife, Jeanette, had to say. She was his world. His everything. And without his family he was nothing. So he lay in bed, staring at the ceiling and hoping that his family would indeed love the house on Mercy Street as much as he did.

Jeanette stirred next to him and threw her arm around his waist. Anthony grabbed it and pulled it towards his mouth. He slid his hand into hers and kissed the back of it. A low moan escaped Jeanette's lips and she smiled sweetly. Anthony leaned over and put his mouth over hers. She accepted his tongue and they made love well into the morning. Outside, a gentle wind stirred the trees. There was another wind waiting to blow somewhere not too far. But that wind would blow through the souls of all that it touched. It would blow until every secret was revealed.

"Good morning," Jeanette said as Anthony opened his eyes.

"Good morning."

Jeanette kissed her husband on the chest and rolled out of bed. Anthony watched her get up, marveling at how well her ass had held up after having two kids. He smiled and Jeanette turned around.

"What are you staring at?" she asked.

Anthony continued smiling and staring at her ass. "I'm just staring at the most beautiful thing in the world," he said.

Jeanette gave her ass a little shake and then went into the bathroom. Anthony rolled over in bed and inhaled deeply. He had to get up. He had to get the kids fed and then maybe, just maybe, all of the stars would be aligned and the whole family would be the proud owners of a new home by the late afternoon. He flung the sheets off and jumped out of bed. He was suddenly invigorated. He pulled on some shorts that had been discarded during the night and headed towards the kids' rooms.

Taylor was already awake when he knocked on her door.

"Come in," Taylor said.

Anthony opened the door and saw his daughter sitting upright on the bed listening to her iPod. "How could you hear me with that thing on?" Anthony asked.

Taylor just smiled and pulled one of her ear buds out. "I hear everything, Daddy. It's a gift."

Anthony smiled back at her. "Well, good. Get dressed. I'm gonna wake up your brother and then make you guys the most magnificent breakfast in all the land."

Taylor giggled and then rolled her eyes. She slid the ear bud back into her ear. Anthony left her door open and then went down the hall to his son's room. The door was already open and his son, Michael, was not in his bed. He leaned his head in and peeked around. "Michael?"

It was quiet. And then a slurping sound came from somewhere near the back of the room. And then a voice spoke. "Daddy!" slurp "Daddy!" slurp.

Anthony acted like he could not be more scared. "Oh no! What horrors await me in this most dirty of rooms?" Anthony said.

Michael jumped out of the closet and roared. Anthony jumped in mock surprise and laughed. "You scared me, son. You're gonna give your old man a heart attack."

Michael came towards his father and gave him a huge hug. "Good morning, Dad."

"Good morning. Get dressed and then head downstairs for breakfast. Got it?"

"Got it," Michael said.

The breakfast was indeed magnificent. Anthony managed to whip up several plates of pancakes with sausage and scrambled eggs. He cut up some fresh fruit for Jeanette and made the kids their own bowl of toppings for their pancakes. He watched his family eat, knowing that part of this special treatment was to butter them up for the rest of the day. Anthony smiled at his pun, knowing that it would take more than just good eats to make them come to his side regarding the house. But why was he even assuming they would need any kind of coaxing? He loved the house at first sight. Maybe they would, too. Right now was not the time to worry about it. He would leave the doubts in the closet before he left. Right now he was more than happy to just be around his family.

"So, are we excited about seeing this new house today?" Anthony asked.

"Does it have a big backyard?" Michael said.

"Oh yeah. Huge! You should have plenty of fun mowing that thing," Anthony said, smiling.

Michael dropped his fork and let out a huge sigh. "Great," he said.

"Just kidding, buddy. But it's a huge property. You'll see."

Taylor swallowed a big helping of eggs and nearly choked. Jeanette patted her on the back. "You okay?" Jeanette asked.

"Fine," Taylor said.

"What time can we see the house?" Jeanette asked.

Anthony looked over at his wife and smiled. He could tell she was starting to get anxious. And that was good. "The realtor told me any time after 11. I said we would probably leave around that time."

"Then I guess we should clean up and go, huh?" Jeanette said.

Anthony stood at the sink cleaning up the last of the dishes. Jeanette was next to him drying off a large serving dish. She seemed deep in thought. Anthony shut off the water and dried his hands. He stood there a moment watching his wife dry the dish, but her mind was clearly elsewhere.

"Something on your mind?" Anthony asked.

Jeanette seemed startled out of her daydreaming and shook her head.

"We have so many great memories in this house. We watched our babies grow up in this kitchen. We made love in every room in this house. A part of me is just a little sad, that's all."

Anthony pulled the serving dish from her hands and set it on the counter. He grabbed his wife and hugged her tight. He was also sad about leaving. But he knew it would be much tougher on her. Men tended to be a little less emotional and attached when it came to things like this. Women held on to ceremony and certain memories could make them cry at the drop of a hat. But Jeanette was right; they had made so many wonderful memories here. Not the least of which was their two children. Anthony held Jeanette out in front of him.

"We're just looking at this house today. No pressure. If you or the kids don't feel the same way I do, then we walk away. We come home and keep looking at houses on the Internet, okay?"

Jeanette nodded. She would keep an open mind about it. She had made her husband that promise. And she intended to keep it.

(3)

They were nearly to Mercy Street when Anthony's cell phone rang. He flipped it open and answered it. "Hello?"

Taylor and Michael were both staring out the window and Jeanette watched her husband try to drive and talk at the same time. She hated cell phones in general, but even more so when people were driving. She hated how easy it was to lose focus on the road and become a much more dangerous driver. And right now, her husband was the guilty party.

"Well, we're almost there, Richard," Anthony said to the phone.

"Oh, okay. No, that's no problem. We'll just look around the grounds if that's okay. See you then." He closed the phone and dumped it into the cup holder on his console. Jeanette was staring at him.

"Richard said that he's just running a little late. We'll just have to snoop around until he gets there." Anthony looked into the rearview mirror and saw his son smiling. "You heard me right, champ. I said snoop. Just like Sam Fisher on that game you and I play."

Michael rolled his eyes. "Maybe you shouldn't try so hard to be cool, Dad. "

"Oh, I don't have to try. I *am* cool," Anthony said, smiling at his son and marveling at how beautiful he was.

A huge copse of trees hung out into the road and obscured any view of the house from the road. Anthony brought the car almost to a complete stop and then eased it onto the gravel path that would lead to the front of the house. He was being dramatic on purpose, but he thought it might lend itself to the magnificence that awaited his family. He felt so strongly about this house and for the first time since he saw it nearly two weeks ago, he wondered why. Why did he want this house with every part of his being? Why did he need his family to love it also? This thought intrigued him. But it also made him have doubts for the very first time. And then the house came into view and all of his worries melted away at the sight of it. He was home.

The Morrisons, Anthony included, all let out a collective sigh when the car made it's way around the trees and the house came into view. Taylor smiled bigger than she could ever remember smiling and Michael made a big O with his mouth that seemed to stay there until they got out of the car. But it was Jeanette that seemed the most amazed. Her eyes lit up like diamonds sparkling in the sunlight. She felt a wave of wonderful warmth sweep through her and in that instant she knew the house was right. It was right for all of them. And of course, Anthony felt the same thing. Had felt it, in fact, nearly two weeks before.

Anthony stopped the car and pulled the keys from the ignition. Taylor was already opening her door. "Wait!" Anthony said. Taylor pulled the door closed. "I just want to tell you guys something real quick," Anthony said.

"What is it, Dad?" Michael asked.

"Just remember, we're here to look. This is not a done deal. If anyone has any reservations about this house, you say it. Cool?"

"Cool."

And then they were out of the car. Michael was scrambling up a small rise that lead to the front porch and Taylor stood near the car for a moment. Anthony went around the car and grabbed Jeanette's hand. She looked at him and smiled.

"This is beautiful," she said.

Anthony only smiled back. He knew it was beautiful. He wouldn't spoil her moment with words. Together they made their way to the front porch.

Michael was half way around the porch when he felt the wind whip up. It felt surprisingly strong for such a sudden gust. But it was real and he felt it whip again as he stood with his back to the house and the whole expanse of the huge backyard in front of him. The wind died down and Michael titled his head like a dog might do when it senses something strange. He continued looking out onto the backyard, but the real action was behind him, in a window set low enough to look into if he had been facing the other way. Another wind swirled and Michael turned around.

"Oh man, did you feel that?" Anthony asked.

"Yeah. That was really strange," said Taylor as she made her way onto the porch.

"Must be coming off the lake," Anthony said.

"There's a lake?" Jeanette asked.

Anthony smiled at her. "Yes there is."

What Michael saw lasted for less than a second. And when it was gone he would not be able to say for sure if he had actually seen it, but for the briefest of moments he thought he saw a goat in the window. And then it was gone. The wind had died down and Michael stood only a moment longer before walking, with a little more speed in his step, towards the front of the house.

"Hey, buddy," Anthony said as Michael came around the corner. "Well, what do you think?"

"It's huge. And where did that wind come from?" Michael asked.

"Probably from the lake."

"There's a lake back there?" Michael said.

"Sure is. But it's back a ways."

Anthony patted his son's head and then made his way around the house. The family followed him. They had just gotten around to the backyard when a horn sounded. It was Richard LeBrock in his Explorer, sounding his horn like some brigadier general rallying the troops to battle. But in this case, it was a rally cry for money. A cry to sell a home that had been vacated under very strange circumstances only two weeks ago. And a cry that might reveal the most intimate secrets of the Morrison family.

They all stood on the porch watching the man get out of his truck. Jeanette looked over at Anthony and nudged his ribs with her elbow. "That's our guy?" she asked.

"Yep," Anthony replied.

Richard LeBrock was a large man. He weighed nearly 250 pounds and had a huge shock of gray hair on his head. He had a jacket slung over his arm and he was lumbering towards them from the gravel drive.

"Good afternoon, folks."

"Good afternoon," the kids replied.

Richard climbed up the steps to the front porch and held his hand out to Anthony.

"Good to see you again, Anthony. And is this the beautiful Mrs. Morrison?'

Anthony gestured towards his wife and she took Richard's outstretched hand.

"It is a pleasure to finally meet you," Richard said.

"Thank you," Jeanette said.

Richard looked down at the two kids and smiled. "And you two must be Taylor and Michael, right?"

The kids smiled back and shook Richard's hand. He knelt down in front of them and put his hands on their shoulders. "What do you guys think of this house?" he asked.

Taylor nodded but Michael hesitated a moment, thinking about what he probably did not see in the window behind the house. "It's really cool," Michael said.

Richard stood up with an audible pop in his knees and laughed.

"Yes it is! Really cool!" Richard said.

They took the path around the back of the house and Richard gave them a brief history of the area. Anthony had heard most of this already, but he watched the expression on his children's faces as Richard told the tale about how the lake behind the property came to be. He smiled when Jeanette gasped at the number of roses that bloomed just behind the shed in late spring. And to think they hadn't even gone into the house yet. So Anthony just watched, occasionally listening, but mostly drifting off into his own little world of thought. He imagined the kids playing in the back yard. He thought of cookouts and camping under the stars on a beautiful autumn evening. He had never felt so attached to anything in his life. Now he could only hope that the rest of his family was falling in love as well. He thoughts returned to the tour with Richard and he noticed that they were already on their way into the back of the house. That way would lead right into the kitchen, he knew. He remembered how wonderful the kitchen was on his first visit. It was so clean and tidy.

Michael had run out in front of the group and was holding open the screen door that lead into the house. Richard unlocked the door and pushed it open. He gestured for everyone to enter and then followed them into the kitchen, just like Anthony remembered.

"Oh my God," Jeanette said.

"It is magnificent. Probably three times the size of most kitchens, I'd bet. And bright, too," Richard said.

It was a bright kitchen. With the entire room running the width of the house, there were eight windows that offered a view on three sides of the house. On a sunny day the room would be positively glowing. Jeanette ran her hands along the marble countertops. "These are beautiful," she said.

"Italian marble, imported in the forties. I only know this because the original owners kept all the paperwork regarding the house. And I mean everything. When we get to the basement I'll show some of the useless receipts and junk that were left behind," Richard said.

Anthony stood in the glow of the sunlight and watched his family look around in awe. He could feel it buzzing in the air like an electric current. They were falling in love already. And they hadn't even gone farther than the kitchen. Anthony moved behind his wife and put a hand in the small of her back. She offered a smile over her shoulder and then continued looking at the cabinets and appliances.

Richard knelt down in front Michael and pulled out a five-dollar bill from his pocket. He held it up to Michael's face. "This is yours if you can tell me how many bedrooms are in this house."

Michael looked over at his father and mother, both of whom just shrugged their shoulders. He looked over at his sister who was not even paying attention. He scrunched up his face and thought hard about the question. "Six," he said.

"Yes!" Richard said. He handed over the money and Michael yelped in excitement.

"Six bedrooms, a family room and formal dining room. There's a huge laundry room with two dryers. There's an office upstairs that looks out onto the property, and there's even a room that the original owners called a library. It's got shelves that line every wall. Enough room to put your entire collection of books. Do you like to read, Michael?"

"I love to read, sir."

"That's great. You guys ready to move on?" Richard asked.

Everyone agreed and they made their way into the living room. Richard pointed out all of the outlets and cable hookups. Jeanette looked around the room and imagined the possibilities. In her mind she was already placing the sofa and love seat. She was arranging the coffee table and even their new 50" HDTV. And as she did this, she started to realize that the problem with this house was not lack of space, but too much of it. There would be large open spaces to walk through and plenty of room to dance and play. It was a good problem to have, she decided.

"I'm amazed at how clean this place is," Jeanette said. "There's not a single mark on the walls or anything."

"Yes, the last owners left this place more than spotless," Richard said.

"What were they like, the last owners?" Anthony asked.

"They were great! It was a family, much like yours. But they had three children. One of their kids was autistic, I think. Anyway, they seemed nice enough. And obviously they were clean." Richard smiled as he said this, as if their cleanliness was a reason to buy in itself. "But enough about them, let's talk about you guys. What do we think so far?"

"I love it," Taylor said. She had been almost invisible up until now. And the whole group seemed to jump a little when she spoke, as if they had forgotten she was even there. Jeanette went to her daughter and kissed her head.

"It is beautiful," Jeanette agreed.

"Great! Shall we move upstairs?" Richard asked.

They all followed him up the long stairway. Michael was in the rear and watching Taylor hop up each step. Her foot caught on one of the steps and she stumbled. Michael giggled. Taylor turned around and punched him in the arm. "Jerk," she said.

A stern look from Jeanette put Michael back on track. They arrived at the top of the stairs and went into a room that was surely the library. Shelves did indeed cover every single open space on the walls. Near the bottom of one shelf, to the right of the door, a stack of magazines was piled up. Michael slid over to the pile and began looking through them. They were all copies of Time, and most from the late seventies.

"Looks like our neat freaks left something behind, eh?" Richard said.

Michael stood up from the pile and turned around to face Richard. "Those are so *old*," he said.

Anthony and Richard laughed at this and Jeanette smiled.

"Anyway, what do think about this room?" Richard asked.

Anthony stood in the middle of the room. He looked around at the walls and imagined all of his books lining those shelves. He imagined sitting up here late at night and sipping on port and reading over a new manuscript. This would be his safe haven to relax and recharge his batteries. He barely gave this room a glance when he had first come to visit the house. He actually forgot all about it. But now, standing here in the middle of it, with his family all around him, was he absolutely sure that this was the house for all of them. A house where they would make new dreams and live out their days as happy as could be. He felt a hand grab his forearm and he was shaken out of his daydreaming.

"You like this, don't you?" Jeanette said, looking at him with her beautiful brown eyes. "This is home, isn't it?"

Anthony didn't know what to say. She had just asked him if this was home. He was sure that she too had fallen in love the way he had when he first came here. Now he just needed to know about the kids. Were they in love yet? Maybe Michael, but Taylor might need a little more convincing. She was always a bit more analytical about things. She never did anything without asking why. And while it could prove to be trying at times, it also offered Anthony a bit of comfort to know that his daughter would look before she leaped. He moved out of the library and stood in the hallway. Rooms stretched out to either side of him and a large bay window offered brilliant sunlight. He held his arms outstretched, palms turned to the ceiling.

"Okay. Pick your bedrooms," Anthony said.

Taylor scrambled out of the library first and went left. Michael was right behind her and turned right. They moved in and out of the rooms, bumping into each other only once. There was giggling and shouts of excitement. Anthony knew this would be the defining moment. If Taylor and Michael bought the excitement of picking out their bedrooms, then they would be sold. And from the sound of things, they were sold.

"This is definitely my room," Taylor said from the doorway of the room she had picked out. Michael emerged from his room moments later.

"And this room . . . is fit for a king."

Jeanette and Richard had joined Anthony in the hallway. They were all smiling, even Richard.

"Mr. And Mrs. Morrison, you have a wonderful family. You should be so proud."

Jeanette felt her eyes well up with tears. "Thank you so much, Richard," she said.

Anthony looked at his wife with sparkles of tears in her eyes. He stared into her eyes and looked for the answer. Jeanette nodded at him and immediately he knew what that answer was. Anthony held out his hand to Richard. "We'll take it."

There were a few more stops on the tour, but in Anthony's mind the deal was sealed on the landing upstairs, near the library and the children's bedrooms. That one look from his wife that told him it was okay to do it. A look that could speak volumes if it should ever be written down. So they went around the rest of the house, smiling and laughing. And when Richard led them to the front of the house again there was a great relief.

"We'll need to discuss a few things before I draw up the paperwork," Richard said.

"What things?" Jeanette asked.

"Mostly clerical things. There will need to be an inspection and all of that stuff. Routine mostly. But it has to be done before any of this goes through. Nothing to be alarmed about, really."

"Anything that might prevent us from getting this house?" Jeanette said.

"Nothing could stop you from getting this house, Mrs. Morrison."

Anthony and Jeanette shared a look of great happiness. Nothing would stop them from getting this house. Nothing at all.

(4)

Michael and Taylor were sleeping. Anthony knew this because he had just checked on them. So he splashed a bit of his cologne on his chest and opened the bathroom door very slow. Jeanette was propped against the headboard of the bed, one leg drawn up to her chest. Anthony glided out of the bathroom and climbed onto the bed. He kissed Jeanette's leg and thigh and her mouth. She kissed him back and they moved together like a tightly wound spring.

"Are the kids sleeping?" Jeanette asked in between kisses.

"Fast asleep," Anthony replied.

"Mr. Morrison, are you trying to seduce me?"

"Yes, Mrs. Morrison. Should I stop?"

"I'll kill you if you stop."

They made love for close to an hour and then sat up in bed sipping on brandy. Jeanette was all smiles and Anthony couldn't help but feel somewhat responsible for that. He had made love to his wife for so long that he knew every inch of her body. He knew the things that made her giggle. And he knew all the right places to touch. It was an art. But now, sitting up in bed in the aftermath of good sex, did he truly feel alive. The day had gone well at the house and it looked like they would be the new owners. The kids had taken warmly to the place, especially Michael. Anthony knew Taylor liked it also, but Michael really seemed to take to it. The most important thing was that they would be able to adapt. They both went to a private school so they would not have to leave their friends until they went into high school. And that was only a year away for Taylor and two more years for Michael. All of the stars seemed to be aligned. And right now, Anthony felt fine.

Jeanette looked over at Anthony and offered him the snifter of brandy. He took it and sipped from it.

"So what exactly do we know about the previous owners?" Jeanette asked.

Anthony was caught off guard by this question. He didn't expect it and sat there with his mouth open for several seconds before responding.

"The previous owners." It was not a question.

"Yeah, you know, the people that lived there before we looked at it."

"Well, I only know what Richard LeBrock told me," Anthony said.

"And that would be?"

"Well," Anthony was choosing his words carefully. He knew next to nothing about the previous owners. But what he did know might seem a little odd to his wife. He certainly didn't want to cause any kind of disruption in her view of things. So he paused and chose his words carefully. "Pretty much the only thing Richard knew was what he learned from the neighbors, the Crays."

Jeanette was getting the impression that Anthony was avoiding the question. He was never evasive like this and something about it bothered her. So she decided to press.

"Okay, hold on. Something is not right. I've asked three different ways now about the previous owners and you've managed to sidestep each question."

"Spoken like a true lawyer," Anthony said.

"I haven't practiced law in almost twelve years. Now answer the question, please."

"Well, not full time. But you have done some consulting over the past several years," Anthony said.

Jeanette glared at him. She was getting angry now. Her husband was willfully dodging a very simple question and she intended to get the answer from him. They rarely argued about anything, but right now Jeanette knew that an argument was coming. Just like a storm brewing in the sky, thunderheads rolling in and lightning cracking far off in the distance. Their storm was also brewing right here in the bedroom. But instead of thunderheads and lightning there would be sharp words and dirty looks. Jeanette threw her legs over the side of the bed and stood up. She did her best work standing on two legs.

Anthony knew what was coming from the moment she glared at him. He had seen that look before and knew it meant trouble. His wife was a firecracker. A woman bent on never losing an argument that she felt strongly about. She practiced law from the moment she graduated from Northwestern University. But Anthony never thought of it as practicing. With Jeanette it was always the thrill of the hunt. She became a shark when she smelled blood and would not let any opportunity pass to shred open a hole in an argument. But she never fought unless she knew she was right. And as much as Anthony did not want to admit it, she was right about this. He did not want to tell her what he knew about the previous owners. Not because he had any juicy details about them, but because so *little* was actually known. What he learned from Richard LeBrock was simply what Richard had learned from Mrs. Cray, the neighbor. Anthony knew he would have to relent to his wife's cross-examination. But he wouldn't do it easily. Lawyer or no lawyer, he still had his pride. This shark would have to earn her blood. Anthony smirked and Jeanette bit.

"You smug jerk," she said. "You know something, but for some reason you're not telling me. Now that can go two ways. One way says that you're not telling me because what you know might make me hesitant about buying this house. But the second way suggests that you might be trying to get a rise out of me; in which case I will not be a party to that. Try as you might, sir, you will not get a rise out of me."

Anthony was suddenly turned on by her talk. She was going into her shark mode and wasn't even aware of it. He marveled at how easily her instincts came to the forefront like the claws of a cat suddenly popping out. She was on to him on both counts and he knew he was fighting a losing battle.

"Well, which one is it?" Jeanette asked.

"Honestly?"

"I can take it," she said.

"It's both. But more the first one than the second one."

Jeanette grabbed the pillow off the bed and threw it at him. "You shit. You're trying to get me worked up, aren't you?"

"Yes."

"But you do know something about the house, don't you?"

"Yes, but it's not as interesting as you might think."

"Don't you think I should be the judge of that?" she asked.

"I suppose, yes."

"Well?" she stared at him, hands on her hips and all attitude.

Anthony grabbed her wrist and pulled her down to the bed. She came reluctantly.

"I'm sorry," he said. "You're just so damn *cute* when you get worked up."

She continued to only stare.

"Okay, okay. Here goes," Anthony said.

(5)

Michael's dream snuck up on him. He was back at the house on Mercy Street, standing on the back porch. To his right was the window where he thought he might have, and then decided that he hadn't, seen the goat. But this time it was night. A large white moon hung in the sky and a terrific shadow crossed the backyard like a crack in the earth. Michael felt calm. He could hear his sister playing somewhere nearby and his mother and father were looking at the lake off in the distance. There was a rustling to his right and he turned.

"Who's there?" he asked.

A pale white face appeared in the window and smiled at him. "Come inside," the face said.

Michael looked around and noticed that his sister was no longer playing and his parents had moved deeper into the distance. He was very much alone. He looked back at the window and saw that the face was gone. And the back door that led into the kitchen was cracked open. Michael felt cold, but he still moved towards the cracked doorway. From somewhere inside, a voice spoke out.

"That's it. Come in here. I want to show you something," the voice said.

And as Michael was about to go through the door, he saw several white faces appear in all of the windows along the back porch. Each one seeming to hang in the air like bizarre ghosts. Michael tried to scream but no sound came out of his mouth.

Michael sat up in bed, startled and afraid. The residue of the dream still hanging on him like sweat. He pulled the covers up to his chin and shuddered. His bedroom was fairly dark, save for a small sliver of moonlight that was filtering in through his cracked blinds. He looked around, eyes growing accustomed to the dark and imagined that the faces from his dream were all around him. That was all he could take. He jumped out of bed and ran down the hall to his sister's room.

Taylor didn't even budge when Michael crawled into bed with her. He pulled himself against her and gave her a hug. And before long, sleep stole over him again.

" . . . ing in my bed?"

That was all Michael caught at first. And then Taylor said it again, louder.

"What are you doing in my bed?" she asked.

Michael sat up and rubbed his eyes. He looked genuinely startled by the question.

"I had a real scary dream. Sorry."

"It's morning. So can you get out of my bed now?"

"Sure. Damn," he said, looking wounded. He got out of her bed and left the room.

Taylor sat on the edge of her bed looking shocked and amazed. "That kid," she said to her empty bedroom.

Everybody wanted something different for breakfast. Michael and Taylor wanted Cheerios, Jeanette felt like an omelet, and Anthony simply wanted a bagel. So they all scrambled around each other, pulling bowls from cabinets and pans from the cupboards. And then they were all sitting around the table, munching on breakfast.

"I know I've asked it a thousand times," Anthony started. "But are we in total agreement on this house?"

They all looked at each other and nodded.

"Good. Then it's settled. Once the inspection gets done this afternoon, and Mr. LeBrock puts the final touches on the paperwork, we'll just need to close. And that could get done in the next week. So in the meantime, I need all of us to go through our stuff and see what we can get rid of. Things we don't need or use anymore. We'll donate the stuff that's still good and trash the junk. Deal?"

"Deal," they all said.

But Jeanette wasn't totally thrilled about the house anymore. Her conversation the night before about why the previous tenants left so quickly had rattled her a bit. And it was nothing she could put her finger on. What Anthony had told her was less than exciting or dramatic. According to the story told by Richard LeBrock, a story passed down from the woman who lived next door, the last owners simply packed up and left in quite a hurry. And as boring as that was, it still poked at her like a sliver stuck just underneath the skin. It was irritating, and she didn't know why. Part of it, she knew, had to do with her apprehension about moving. That was stressful in itself. But now she had something else to worry about. She looked around at her family and marveled at how happy they all looked. And that alone would be worth the worry. Even if it turned out that she had nothing to worry about at all.

Anthony pushed himself away from the table and stretched. "I have to go into the office for a few hours today," he said.

"Aw, dad. You said we would go see a movie today," Michael said.

"Well, the publishing world doesn't always work on our schedule, son. I have a few manuscripts to finish up and then I'll meet with Mr. LeBrock for the inspection. And then, while I'm gone, you guys can all get your stuff together. If all goes well, we'll be moving in the next couple of weeks."

Taylor and Michael smiled and high-fived across the table. Jeanette smiled also.

"And tonight, when I get home, we can catch a movie," Anthony said.

"Yeah!" Michael said. "Can we go see the new *Die Hard* movie?"

"What's it rated?" Anthony asked.

"PG-13."

"And how old are you?' Anthony said.

"Eleven."

"So the answer is?"

Michael looked disappointed at first but turned all smiles when his dad stood up and winked at him. He knew that wink. It meant that they would probably watch the new *Die Hard* movie after all. His sister and mother would not be happy about it, but he would be thrilled. A small victory. Michael finished his breakfast.

Anthony flipped open his phone and pulled up Richard LeBrock's number. He hit the dial button and waited while it rang. The traffic on the 408 was lighter than usual and Anthony could not have been happier. He hated taking this route to his office, but it was the shortest. Richard answered.

"Richard. It's Anthony Morrison. How are you?"

"I'm fine. What's happening?"

"Well, I just wanted to make sure we were still on for this afternoon. For the inspection?"

"Yes, sir. I figured I would just meet you at the house," Richard said.

"That sounds great."

"I have something I need to ask you, Anthony," Richard said.

"Go ahead."

"Well, after we toured the house with your family the other day, the neighbor, Mrs. Cray, called me on the phone."

"Okay," Anthony said, recalling the conversation he had the night before with his wife.

"It's kind of an odd request, but she asked if she could meet you. I told her I would ask you."

"I suppose it's normal for a neighbor to want to know who's moving in next door," Anthony said.

"So should I set it up for today, after the inspection?" Richard asked.

"Sure. That's fine."

"She really is a great old woman. The whole family for that matter. Really nice people," Richard said.

"Okay, I'll see you this afternoon. Bye," Anthony hung up and went back to his drive. He really didn't have a problem meeting this woman, but it was strange that she called his realtor to set up a meeting. Couldn't she just wait until they moved in to talk to him? Or was there something more she wanted to say about the people that lived in the house before? Anthony wasn't up for dark secrets. He never did like that. But he had a hunch that today he might get a small dose of what he didn't want. He turned on his exit and drove the rest of the way to his office in a cloudy haze of doubt and wonder. Doubt, for the first time, about the house. And wonder about what Mrs. Cray had to say to him.

(6)

Jeanette yanked a shopping cart from the long line of interlocked carts. She swiveled around and made her way towards the produce. She was nearly to the first bin, filled with onions of every size and color. She pulled a red one off the pile and looked at it. Seemingly satisfied, she pulled a plastic bag from the spindle and tossed the onion in it. It was as she was moving away from the onion bin that the hand settled on her shoulder. Jeanette turned around quickly and found herself face to face with an older woman.

"Hello there," the woman said.

"Hi," Jeanette replied.

"I'm sorry to startle you. My name is Harriet Cray. I live in the other house on Mercy Street."

It took Jeanette a moment to register what the woman had just said. There were only two houses on Mercy Street, and one of them was the house that she and her family had looked at only yesterday. So that meant that this older woman was Mrs. Cray, just like she had said. Jeanette blushed.

"I am so sorry. It took me a minute to register exactly what you were talking about. I'm Jeanette Morrison."

Jeanette held out her hand and Harriet shook it.

"It's so very nice to meet you," Harriet said.

"So, how can I help you?" Jeanette asked.

"Well, this is more of a coincidence. I don't usually shop on this side of town. We have a local grocer near the house," Harriet said.

Jeanette only listened. She felt a strange sense of calm as this woman spoke to her. It was as if her words were lulling Jeanette to sleep.

"So anyway, like I said, this is more of a coincidence. And I figured that since you were here, I should do the neighborly thing and introduce myself."

"Yes, that is very kind. But forgive me for asking. How did you even know what I looked like?" Jeanette asked.

"Oh, I saw your whole family when you came to take a look at the house. Handsome children, by the way."

"Well, thank you. That's very kind," Jeanette said. But something bothered her about this. The two houses on Mercy Street were not close enough together to get a good view of anything, let alone someone's face. And that would mean that Harriet Cray was a lot closer than her living room window when she got a good look at her family. And that suggested a very nosy neighbor. A nosy neighbor indeed. And that was something that Jeanette did not care for one bit.

"I sure hope you don't mind my saying say so, Mrs. Morrison, but your son is especially striking."

But she did mind her saying so. Minded very much, in fact. This whole situation had taken on an air of weird energy and Jeanette was growing more uncomfortable by the minute. Jeanette wanted to end this conversation as quickly as possible. But she also wanted to ask a question or two about the previous tenants.

"Could I ask you a question, Mrs. Cray?"

"Of course," Harriet said.

"Why did the last owners of the house we were looking at leave so suddenly?"

"Ah, that seems to be the hot question, no? It seems that everyone wants to know that answer. Didn't your realtor, Mr. LeBrock, fill you in?"

"He told us next to nothing, quite frankly," Jeanette said. She thought about how Mr. LeBrock had told HER nothing at all. It was her husband who had filled her in.

"Well, that's about all there is to tell."

"Did you meet these people?" Jeanette asked.

"Oh yes. They were very sweet. Much like your own family. But I think they might have had a problem with the darn wind."

Jeanette suddenly remembered standing outside of the house yesterday afternoon and marveling at how suddenly that gust of wind had come through and then was totally gone again. She thought it odd that Harriet had brought this up. "The wind?"

"Oh yes. It can get terribly strong sometimes. And when it blows it feels like it's going right through you. Right through your soul."

This caused Jeanette to shudder. The way this woman had put so much emphasis on the last word. Your Soul. It was almost too much to bear. Jeanette cleared her throat and thought how to best end this conversation.

"Harriet, it was a great pleasure to meet you. We have the inspection on the house today, so perhaps we will see each other soon."

"Oh yes. In fact, I invited your husband over to chat this afternoon, after the inspection."

"Really," Jeanette said.

And with that they parted ways and Jeanette finished her shopping. But her head was never fully away from the conversation with Harriet Cray. She couldn't get the woman's words out of her mind. They hung there like dead snake skins, drying out and falling apart in her mind. Until there was only genuine uneasiness. She paid for the groceries and pushed her cart out of the store. As soon as she was outside she pulled out her cell and called Anthony. He had some explaining to do.

"Why didn't you tell me that Harriet Cray was meeting you this afternoon?"

"First of all, hello. Secondly, I only just found out myself. And third, she invited Richard and myself over after the inspection. Is there a problem?"

Jeanette was pushing the cart at a clip. The phone was fumbling around on her shoulder and she nearly lost it before grabbing it and holding it to her ear.

"You're damn right there's a problem. She just saw me at the grocery store. Apparently she doesn't even shop there, but she made a point of coming to meet me. That's a bit strange, wouldn't you say?"

"I suppose," Anthony said on the other end.

"You suppose? What kind of person goes twenty miles out of their way to say hello to a potential new neighbor? Who does that?"

"Sounds like Mrs. Cray does that, honey."

"Dammit, Anthony. Why are you so calm about this?"

"I don't see a problem. She certainly seems a bit eccentric, but I wouldn't get all worked up just because she made a point to meet you in a grocery store that's out of her way."

"Okay, you know what . . . just have a great day!" Jeanette slammed her phone closed and unlocked the car doors. She threw the groceries in the back and then got into the driver's seat. She had to take a deep breath. The conversation with her husband had left her angry and confused. She couldn't figure why she was so upset. It took only a moment to find calm and then she settled in for the drive home.

Jeanette and Anthony rarely argued. And when they did it was usually like the argument she had just had with him on the phone. They rarely stayed mad at each other for longer than an hour and when something was bothering one or the other they would talk about it. She knew that was why they stayed happily married for the past thirteen years. Marriage was work, but it was also the most rewarding kind of work. You just had to continue to work at it. It was series of compromises that sometimes made you do things against your better judgment. And right now, buying the house on Mercy Street was against her better judgment. But she would bite her tongue. Strange old lady or not, her kids really liked the house. And truth be told, so did she. The houses were far enough apart that she hoped she wouldn't have to spend too much time seeing the Cray woman. But then again, if this woman was willing to drive twenty miles out of her way, a little walk down the lane would not be much of a problem. Right now Jeanette just wanted to get home and hug her children. She missed them terribly.

(7)

Peter Siegelman poked his head into Anthony's office. He knocked on the door with two knuckles and Anthony looked up from his desk.

"Sorry to bother you, Mr. Morrison. But the boss man wants to see you in his office." Peter said. He waited until Anthony stood up before turning around and leaving.

Anthony shook his head clear. He had no idea why his boss, Jonah Castle, wanted to see him. Anthony rarely saw anyone during his day. He kept to his office, mostly. He had been in the publishing business for a long time. And he was only now at the point where he could shut his door and not be bothered for several hours. And the boss NEVER called for him like this. If anything, the phone on his desk would beep and a pretty voice would let him know that someone was looking for him. But the boss never sent someone like Peter Siegelman to fetch him. Peter worked in an office on the opposite side of the building. He was in charge of layout and design. It was a job that Anthony was very thankful he never learned. It required long hours and tight deadlines and those were things that Anthony despised. Not because he was lazy, but because he put a premium on the time he had with his family. And working in Layout and Design allowed him very little time with the people he loved the most.

Anthony made his way to Jonah's office and peeked in the windows with the partially closed blinds. The boss was in there with his secretary. They were laughing as Jonah tickled her. Anthony thought that Mrs. Castle might not approve of this. So Anthony coughed rather loudly and knocked on the door. Moments later the pretty secretary opened the door and walked out past Anthony. He watched her go and then made his way into Jonah Castle's office.

"Hello, Anthony," Jonah said. "Please, have a seat."

Anthony sat in a large chair in front of the desk. "Good morning, sir," Anthony said.

"Peter Siegelman over in Layout tells me you're buying the house out on Mercy Street. That right?"

"Boy, word travels fast, huh?" Anthony said.

"It sure does. And in this business that's not just a pun. Anyway, how have you been?" Jonah asked.

"I'm doing very well, thanks. Jeanette's great, the kids are thrilled to be out of school."

"I'm sure. So what exactly do you know about that house you're buying?"

Anthony thought it odd how jarring this conversation was. It was as if Jonah could not get to the subject of the house fast enough. All the small talk seemed to irritate him. And then another thought came to him. Why did the house have such an interesting history that everyone seemed to know about it? Anthony had never heard about the house before he went to see it. He had never heard stories of any kind until only recently. And the things he had heard were pretty boring. He shifted in his chair and cleared his throat.

"Well, the only thing I know is what I saw," Anthony said. "And I've got to tell you, I fell in love with that house at first sight."

"Well, that all's fine and dandy, but what do you *know* about it?" Jonah asked again.

Anthony wanted to scream. Why was this conversation so odd? And at what point did any of this seem important enough to be summoned into the boss's office to have this discussion. Anthony squirmed uncomfortably in his chair. The room seemed to grow warmer and he wished that Jonah's secretary would come in and tell the boss that he had an important phone call. Anything to get out of this room.

"It's an odd question," Anthony said. "What should I know about the house?"

"I only wonder if your realtor explained the history of the place. There's certainly a rich history out on Mercy Street. One that pertains to your ethnic history." Jonah said.

There it was. Anthony had spent the better part of his professional career avoiding the pitfalls and hazards that came with being a black man in corporate America. But he worked for a publishing house. A place that catered to every type of book under the sun. And that included very successful black authors as well. But now, sitting across from his boss, was he reminded of just how close to the surface racial tension boiled. And yet Jonah had said nothing that was rude or racial at all. But he had brought it up nonetheless. And right now that was enough.

He had done his best to raise his children to be colorblind. He and Jeanette made a conscious decision to leave their own beliefs at the door and teach their kids only one thing. And that thing was love. They didn't discuss anything in terms of black or white. They simply talked about people. And Anthony thought that they had done a great job of it. Michael and Taylor were stable, well-rounded children. They did well in school and never got into serious trouble. The world was far from perfect or racially unbiased, but he felt like they were doing their part to eliminate it from the world. But Jonah wanted to tell him something about his ethnic history.

"Like I said, sir, the house just moved me when I saw it."

"Maybe I shouldn't be the one to tell you this. Maybe you should ask around and discover it for yourself. But I feel like I owe it to you to mention it." Jonah said.

"Okay."

"That property, the one with your house on it, used to be a plantation. A slave plantation." Jonah said.

Anthony's throat locked up. He wanted to ask a thousand questions all at once and get to the bottom of this. But why hadn't Richard LeBrock told him? He knew why. He knew that Anthony would probably not want to hear that part of the story. And while the idea of living in a former slave home did not bother him, the fact that Richard LeBrock left out such an important detail did.

"Jonah, how do you know all of this?" Anthony asked.

"I'm curious. We are in the book business after all, and I love to read. I'm especially interested in the history of our town here. Our town and the surrounding little neighborhoods that make up most of where we live. So when I heard that you and your family had been down to that house, I thought I should speak with you about it. Simply to see if you had been given all of the info."

"So beyond the fact that the house used to contain slaves, was their anything else odd about it?" Anthony said. He could feel himself calming down. Jonah did not call him in here to harass him. He simply wanted to share what he knew about the house. Anthony now thought that was rather kind of the man. A bit odd, but kind.

"Depends on what you consider odd, Anthony."

Anthony thought that comment itself was odd, and he smiled in response. If this was happening at work, with his boss, he could only imagine what kind of fun was going to be had with Mrs. Cray later on this afternoon. And then there was his wife to deal with later. His day looked to be very interesting indeed.

"Well, to be honest, Jonah, this whole conversation is odd. But I suppose you mean with the house. So I guess anything you tell me about it will strike me as a bit off."

"I can tell you what I know if that suits you. I'll tell you everything. After all, I'm not trying to sell you a house," Jonah said.

"I'd be lying if I said I wasn't curious."

"Are you thirsty?" Jonah asked.

"Very," Anthony said.

(8)

Michael and Taylor were playing cards in the living room. Michael was waging war with a stack full of aces and Taylor was getting more than a little aggravated. They had been sitting here for nearly a half hour and nothing seemed to be changing. So Taylor flipped the last card in her stack. It was an ace. Michael flipped a king and Taylor howled in excitement.

"This is the beginning of the end for you, little bro." She said.

"You have two cards," Michael said.

"Yes, but two very good cards. Just keep flipping, sucker."

And sure enough, it wasn't long before Taylor's stack was growing. She pulled another ace from a war that she won. Things were starting to look up.

"So why were you in my bed this morning?" Taylor asked.

"I had a really bad dream,"

"Yeah, you said that. But what was it about?" she said.

"I was standing in the back of the new house. And then there were these creepy faces in the windows and a voice asked me to come into the house. I don't remember much more than that. I know when I woke up I was really creeped out though. So that's why I had to hop into your bed."

Taylor nodded as if she understood. She loved her brother, but she did not enjoy him sleeping in her bed. They were too old for that now. But she loved him very much, and if he needed a little comforting she was happy to help him. She won another war and took another ace from his arsenal. He cringed at this.

"Do you think we'll end up getting that house, Taylor?"

"Of course. Why wouldn't we?"

"Just wondering. Maybe we should start going through our stuff, like Dad asked." Michael said.

"Yeah. And besides, you're about to get your butt kicked in this game. I told you it was the beginning of the end."

Michael flipped the last two cards in his stack and stood up. Taylor gathered up the cards with an immense grin on her face.

They met in the kitchen and grabbed some Triscuits. Cleaning out their rooms would be hard work. They would need a snack. Mom might have a fit about eating in their rooms, but they would counter that with the argument that at least they were cleaning their rooms. And if all else failed, they would give their mom a big hug and tell her how much they loved her. That usually did the trick. Parents were suckers for a well-placed hug. Michael went upstairs to his room. Taylor hung back in the kitchen. She was putting some peanut butter on Triscuits when the phone rang. She answered it quickly, smearing a small bit of peanut butter on the receiver.

"Hello?" she said.

"Hi, sweetie. Whatcha doin?"

"Oh, hi Mom. Michael and I were just getting ready to go through the stuff in our rooms."

"Very good. I just got done at the grocery. So I should be home shortly. Has your father called at all?"

"No. Why?" Taylor said.

"Just curious. You two behave, got it?'

"Yes, Mom. Love you."

"Love you too."

Taylor clicked the phone off and set it on the counter. She went back to her crackers and filled a plate with a dozen Triscuits smeared with peanut butter. She had just grabbed the plate and was heading out of the kitchen when the phone rang again. She set down the plate and answered.

"Yes?"

There was a pause before anyone answered.

"Hello?" Taylor said.

"Hi. May I speak to Michael Morrison please?" It was a woman's voice. And Taylor thought it sounded like an older woman.

"Uh, sure. Could you hold on, please?"

"Okay," the woman said.

Taylor picked up the plate with one hand and kept the phone in the other. She walked upstairs and found Michael sitting on the floor near his closet. He had already pulled most of the contents of his closet out and was sitting with stuff piled all around him. He looked dwarfed by it. Taylor giggled and held the phone out to him.

"It's for you," she said.

"Who is it?"

"I don't know, booger. Just take it."

Michael did his best to stand up and grabbed the phone.

"Hello?' he said.

"Is this Michael Morrison?" the woman's voice asked.

"Yes. And who's this?" he asked.

"No thank you," the woman said.

And then there was a click. Michael pulled the phone from his ear and stared at it.

"Well, who was it?" Taylor asked, still standing in the doorway with her plate of Triscuits.

"I don't know. She asked if I was Michael Morrison, and then she said 'No thank you.'"

"Weird," Taylor said. She turned and left the doorway. Michael stood there only a moment longer, still looking at the phone. He clicked it off and set it on his bed. And by the time he settled back into his pile of junk on the floor he had already forgotten about the conversation on the phone. He would not remember it for several weeks. And when he did remember it, it would scare him to his core.

(9)

Anthony pulled into the driveway of the house on Mercy Street. Richard was already standing on the front porch waiting for him. A woman was standing near Richard. Anthony assumed it was the inspector. He knew that this part of the home buying process was tedious and boring, but he also knew that it was a necessary evil. And if the inspector found anything that could potentially hurt his family, he wanted to know about it. So Anthony killed the engine and got out. Richard waved to him as he made his way to the porch.

"Good afternoon, Anthony," Richard said.

Anthony waved back. "Hello."

The woman standing next to Richard held out her hand as Anthony approached.

"This is Gayle Lamotta, Anthony. She'll be handling the inspection." Richard said.

"Nice to meet you," Gayle said.

"Gayle, why don't you get started. I need to go over a few things with Mr. Morrison."

The two men stood where they were until Gayle was in the house.

"We'll be right there, Gayle," Richard said.

When she was out of sight Richard pulled Anthony by the arm and guided him around to the back of the house.

"What's going on, Richard?" Anthony asked.

"I just wanted to make sure you were okay. I saw your face the moment you pulled up. You look a little pale." Richard laughed, hoping his little joke hadn't offended Anthony.

Anthony smiled back, knowing that Richard was just trying to be funny. But a black man going pale was a funny thing indeed. Anthony kept smiling, but inside he kept turning the conversation with Jonah over in his head. Jonah had filled him in on everything he thought was worth mentioning. There was a long history in this house. A history that included slavery and possibly murder. But that didn't really trouble Anthony all that much. What bothered him was that his Realtor had failed to mention it. But Anthony could tell that Richard was aware of something. He thought he might try and get it out of him. Make him sweat a little.

"I get it. A black man going pale. That's funny."

Richard looked suddenly very uncomfortable.

"Speaking of being black, when were you going to tell me about the house, Richard?"

"Anthony, this is something I myself only found out a few days ago."

"Right. And my family and I were here yesterday. So that means that you knew about it then. Right?"

"You're right, Anthony. But I certainly didn't want to bring it up in front of the children."

"Well, that's very noble," Anthony said.

Richard was looking everywhere but in Anthony's eyes. He looked troubled and more than a little sad. He looked ready to say something when Anthony held up a hand to stop him.

"Please. I know you have a job to do. Your job is to sell us this house. And I want you to know that barring some terrible structural flaw that gets found today, I WILL be buying this house. My family and I love the house. But I want every bit of info on this property since it was first built. I want any court papers. I want any deeds that got lost in the shuffle of bureaucratic bullshit."

Richard looked up when Anthony cursed, a look of very real shock on his face.

"Am I clear on this, Richard?"

"Yes. And I'm truly sorry you had to find out like this. And if I can ask, how did you find out about it?" Richard said.

"My boss says he's into the history of this town. He heard I was looking at the property and thought I should know about it, me and my family being black and all."

Anthony could see the look on Richard's face. It was almost comical.

"Yeah, I know. You're not used to me talking like this, are you? I just want you to know how unhappy I am about how I found out. I don't mince my words, Richard," Anthony said.

Gayle Lamotta came out of the doorway that led into the kitchen. She finished writing something on her clipboard and looked up at Richard and Anthony.

"I'm heading upstairs. Would you like to join me?" she asked.

Anthony gave Richard one final look to make sure he understood. The look that came back said that he understood completely. And that was good because Anthony felt like he was in charge again. He wanted this house and had every intention of getting it. Something told him that his life would change once he got the house. And that seemed like an exciting prospect.

The inspection finished up nearly an hour later. Anthony shook the hands of Gayle and Richard and stood on the porch as they got into Richard's vehicle.

"You sure you don't want me to come with you?" Richard asked.

"I'm positive. I think Mrs. Cray might be more open if you're not around. But I appreciate it. I'll call when I'm done. Then maybe you and I can compare notes."

"Very well. And congratulations, Anthony. We'll close on the house in two weeks."

Richard and Gayle drove away. Anthony waved at them and then just stood on the porch for another minute or so. He liked how the gentle breeze whirled through the trees in the front yard. It wasn't a wind like the other day, but a gentle flow of warm air. He looked to his right and saw the Cray house off in the distance. Their house looked much like this one. Much like HIS house. He smiled as the realization dawned on him that this was now going to be his home. All of the nonsense that seemed to come about over the last few days was rolling away behind the beauty of the house itself. He didn't care what it had once been used for. He knew his heritage. He knew the struggle that his people had gone through. But he also felt like the greatest accomplishment was in owning this house as a free man. Where there had once been slaves there was now a successful black man and his family. One more bit of business with this Mrs. Cray woman and then he would go home and deal with his wife. He knew she was now probably calm and rational. He would tell her about what he learned today. He would tell her because he kept no secrets from her. Almost no secrets. Everyone had secrets, he decided.

The wind picked up as he made the walk up the lane to the Cray house. It was a wind that lifted his shirt and forced him to tuck it in. It seemed to be coming from his back, from his new house. And just as he reached the front porch of the Cray house it whipped up with such ferocity that he nearly lost his balance. He jumped up onto the porch and was about to knock when the door swung open and a short older woman greeted him.

"Hello there. You must be Anthony Morrison."

"Yes, ma'am. How are you?"

"I'm very well. Won't you come in.?" she said.

Anthony stepped into the house and was greeted by a strong smell of warm apples. It was a wonderful smell and it reminded him of his own grandmother who used to bake pies all year long from the fresh fruit that grew out in her yard.

Harriet Cray held out her hand and Anthony shook it gently. "Harriet Cray," she said.

"Mrs. Cray I must tell you, it smells divine in here. Are you baking something?"

"Harriet, please. And yes I am. I'm baking apple turnovers."

"I knew it! My grandmother used to bake and it smells just like her place, when she was alive."

"I bet she was a lovely cook."

"Yes, ma'am. Grandma's food is always just a little bit better, isn't it."

"Enough of this ma'am stuff. You call me Harriet or I'm going to send you out of here without any of my turnovers.

"You got it, Harriet."

They moved into the living room and sat down. Anthony noticed all of the antique decorations. She had old statues and large claw-footed furniture. Knit blankets were laid over the couch and love seat. It was warm and cozy in here and Anthony felt very comfortable.

"Are you thirsty?" Harriet asked.

"No thank you. I can't stay long. I just wanted to share a few minutes of your time." Anthony said.

"Well, since it was me who invited you, I guess I should just get down to it." She said.

"Fair enough," Anthony said.

"How did your inspection go?"

"Very well. The house seems to be in great shape."

"So that means that you'll be buying it?" she asked.

"It appears so."

"Well, I feel like I should share a few things with you then. Things that Mr. LeBrock might have forgotten to mention."

"Harriet I have to tell you, I was informed of some things only just today. And I have to admit that I was taken aback by them."

"I assume you're talking about the slavery?" she asked.

"Yes."

"That's all true, but there's more. There are things about the folks who used to live in that house. The ones who moved out rather quickly."

Anthony wasn't sure what she might have to tell him, but the air suddenly grew heavy. He could still smell the warm apples, but the smell seemed less comforting now.

"Okay," Anthony said. It was all he could think to say.

"I knew the family that lived there. I knew them only briefly, of course. They only stayed for about two weeks. But I talked to the wife mostly. She was a kind woman. She loved her children very much and seemed to have a good relationship with her husband.

He was a kind enough fellow. And the children were wonderful. One of them was autistic."

Anthony remembered Richard mentioning this when they looked at the house only yesterday.

"Anyway, they seemed very kind. But one night-probably the last night they slept in that house-I saw the wife come running from the house screaming. And I don't mean angry screaming. I mean terrified screaming."

Anthony wondered what would make a woman run from that house screaming. He also wondered why Richard had failed to mention this part of the story as well.

"Mr. LeBrock didn't mention this to me," Anthony said.

"I didn't tell him that part of the story. I only told him I saw the woman outside of her house. And from this distance, that was all I saw. Richard didn't press me on it. He simply nodded, much like you're doing now, and listened."

Anthony inhaled deeply. "Why tell me any of this, Harriet? Why let me in on such a strange story unless it has something to do with me and my family?"

"None of it has anything to do with you . . . yet," she said.

The look on Anthony's face told her to proceed. "But the moment you move into that house, then it becomes your problem."

Anthony knew he would have to choose his words very carefully. He didn't want to come off angry, but this conversation was starting to annoy him. It felt like Harriet Cray was trying to convince him not to buy the house. He wasn't sure if that was the case, but if it were he would get to the bottom of it.

"Are you talking about ghosts?" Anthony asked.

Harriet looked taken aback by the question, as if even asking it was absurd.

"Not ghosts, Mr. Morrison. But the very foundations of your soul."

He had absolutely no idea what that meant. What exactly was the foundation of his soul and what did any of that have to do with the house.

"Harriet, you have been a very kind host, but I feel like I should be going."

"I've upset you, haven't I?" she asked.

"I'm just confused as to why you asked to meet me."

"I thought you should know what you were getting into, that's all."

"The only thing I know is how confusing this all is. You mentioned the foundation of the soul. I couldn't tell you what that means. So I'm going. It was very nice meeting you." Anthony stood up and prepared to leave.

Harriet spoke just as he got to the door. He paused.

"You asked me if there were ghosts," Harriet said.

"Then what made that woman run from the house in such a panic, Harriet?"

"The truth, Mr. Morrison."

"The truth," he said.

"When the wind blows through that house, the truth is always revealed."

And that's how their conversation ended. Anthony was no closer to understanding what any of that meant, but he knew that he wanted to distance himself from the Cray house as much as possible. He drove away from Mercy Street faster than he should have and kept up the pace until he was back on the highway heading home to his wife and children. He hoped they were doing well. He had promised his son a night out at the movies and he intended to deliver. But the thoughts that swirled through his head were all about the house. And Mrs. Cray. Anthony wondered for the first time why he hadn't seen Mr. Cray. And didn't Richard mention that they had kids? Whatever their familial status, Anthony felt odd about the whole afternoon. What started with a revealing conversation with his boss turned even stranger when he met the Cray woman. He could only hope that Jeanette was not still mad at him. If she were, he would deal with it. Just like he always did. And then he would sit his family down one last time and make sure that they wanted to move into the house. He knew he did. He had never wavered on that. Even when Jonah spilled the beans about the slaves, Anthony still wanted the house. He would tell

Jeanette everything and then hope she was as understanding as he was. If not, he would call Richard LeBrock in the morning and back out of the deal. It was as simple as that.

(10)

Jeanette greeted him with a big hug and Anthony knew right away that she was not mad. He hugged her back, holding her even after she tried to pull away.

"I love you," he whispered in her ear.

"I love you too, sweetie," she said, pinching his ass and biting his earlobe.

Michael and Taylor were sitting at the kitchen table playing Clue. Anthony gave them both a kiss and then sat next to Taylor. He put his arm around her shoulder.

"Would you guys mind going out side for a little bit. I want to talk to mom."

"Uh oh, what did you do now, Mom?" Taylor said as she stood up and walked out the back door into the yard. Michael shook his head and followed his sister. When they were out of the room Anthony pulled Jeanette down to the table. She sat down next to him. She looked worried.

"What is it?" she asked.

"I met with the Cray woman. She mentioned a few things. Nothing big." Anthony had no intention of telling Jeanette about the conversation with Harriet. He thought it would do more harm than good and thought better of having a discussion about souls and ghosts and the truth. So he simply glossed over it. But he would tell her about what his boss told him. She had a right to know that at least.

"Okay, and what else?" she said.

"This is the big one, I'm afraid. I learned today that the house used to be a slave property."

"Slave property? You mean slaves owned it?" she asked.

"No. It was a plantation. Slaves worked and lived there."

"Sweetie, I hate to bring it up, but Slavery's been abolished for a long time now. That would make that house VERY old. And it certainly doesn't look old enough."

"I'm sure renovations have taken place over the years, Jeanette. But this is what was told to me by Jonah. And then later, when I confronted Richard LeBrock about it, he confirmed it."

Jeanette was weighing her words carefully. She knew this was probably hard for Anthony to say. She knew how badly he wanted the house. And also how badly he wanted his family to love the house. So she thought a moment before responding.

Finally, she said, "Did you think I would change my mind about the house when you told me this?"

"I honestly wasn't sure what you'd say. I just knew that I owed it to you to hear it from me now, before you heard it later from someone else."

She paused again, knowing that in her heart she wanted to move into that house. She truly did. And while it was noble of her husband to give her the straight story, she couldn't help but feel like one small piece of the puzzle was missing. Any couple that spends a considerable amount time together eventually learns how to read their mate. It's a natural thing that makes lying become harder and harder as the years pass. And while Jeanette did not think Anthony was lying to her, she did think that maybe there was one small bit of info that he may have left out. She also knew that pressing it right here and now would be futile. He had no intention of giving up anything else, of that she was sure. So for now she would simply assure him that the decision to buy the house was a good one. And she truly believed that.

"We can argue about the year slavery was abolished in our new home. And then maybe we can solve world hunger while we're at it."

She smiled at him and Anthony knew the conversation was over. The decision had been made final right here at the kitchen table. Anthony had never loved his wife more than he did right at this moment. And as his children yelled and screamed out in the yard, Anthony leaned over and kissed his wife. He felt very happy.

The two weeks to the closing passed without incident. Anthony and Jeanette cleaned their own closets and donated a large portion of their stuff to Goodwill. Taylor and Michael did the same. They decided to keep both of the kids beds and their own, but they would donate the couches and tables in the living room and buy new stuff when they moved in. All in all, it was uneventful and satisfying at the same time.

When the moment came for Anthony to meet Richard LeBrock at his office to sign the paperwork, it was a simple affair. They signed the papers and then Richard shook Anthony's hand.

"Congratulations," he said.

"Thank you, Richard. Listen, I'm sorry about losing my cool back at the house a few weeks ago. That's not like me."

"I have to admit, hearing you curse was a bit exciting," Richard said.

"Well, I'm not sure exciting is the word. But I am sorry if I was more than a little rude."

"No worries. I should have told you all that I knew. In any case, the house is yours. I wish your family the best, Mr. Morrison."

"We'll talk to you in a few weeks, when we're ready to sell the place," Anthony said, smiling.

Richard turned sharply and gave Anthony a very surprised look. "Not funny, Mr. Morrison."

But Anthony thought it was just about the funniest thing in the world.

(11)

The end of summer was drawing to a close and Michael and Taylor began to complain about going back to school. The warmth of summer still lingered, but the nights became cooler and less humid. Anthony and Jeanette were finally beginning to settle in to the new place. They had done some minor touch-up work around the house. They cleaned baseboards and repainted a few of the rooms. The basement was left for last.

Anthony knew he would have to deal with it eventually. But a part of him was actually worried about what he might find down there. Not dead bodies or ghosts, but what kind of information was stored down there. What kind of secrets would he find? So one afternoon, after playing catch with Michael in the backyard, he kissed Jeanette on the cheek and told her he was heading downstairs to tackle the basement. She asked if she could help him, but he declined. He wanted to see for himself. Partly because he wanted to be left alone for a few hours, but also because he wanted to be able to keep any secrets he found to himself. He knew that anything odd might upset the family, and so far nothing had gone wrong in the house. They had been in there for almost a month now and nothing was odd. In fact, Mrs. Cray only came over twice. Once, she was simply saying hello. And the other time she just happened to be walking by when they were all out in the front yard. And both visits were short. Anthony felt like they had set some unspoken boundaries that Harriet Cray was respectful of. Either way, it had been an uneventful month.

So Anthony took his cup of iced coffee downstairs and stood amidst the pile of boxes that littered the walls. He knew this would be a job that might take several weeks to truly sort out. But it also felt like an adventure. He looked around and found an old wooden stool under the stairs. He pulled it out and sat down. Then he grabbed the nearest box and dug in.

Most of the boxes in the basement were theirs. They used it for storage, obviously, but also as a place to put boxes that no one wanted to empty just yet. Taylor had a box of stuffed animals down here that she swore she would want opened but had yet to touch. Michael had three boxes of books, each labeled as to its contents, which was already overgrown with cobwebs. Anthony knew those boxes might stay down in the basement for quite a while. But the other boxes-the ones not labeled by his family-were the ones he was interested in. They would hold the mystery that he had suddenly grown so interested in finding out about.

So he grabbed a box closest to where he was sitting and looked it over. It was not labeled but the design on the side of box suggested it used to hold Cherry Tree Apples, WA. Anthony had never heard of Cherry Tree Apples. He could have cared less. So he ripped open the top flap and began going through the contents. What he found was less than mysterious.

There was an old scarf on top. It was a dull, faded red and looked like it had seen a few winters. Underneath the scarf was a porcelain pig. The pig had an apron on that said Makin' Bacon. Anthony smiled as he pulled the pig from the box. He gave it a look and then set it down on the ground next to him. At the bottom of the box was an old record. It was an old Prince record, For You. The cover showed Prince in all his afro-haired glory, spread out across a brown and gold landscape. Anthony knew the album well. He had grown up in the late seventies when Prince was a rising star. He remembered the song Soft and Wet and smiled as he thought about that. He pulled the record from the box and held it up like a sacred relic. He only wished he still had a record player. He might play the grooves out of the damn thing if he did.

A second box revealed some more clothing-mostly winter things-and a book about insects. Anthony wondered why these things were left behind. And which family did they belong to. He knew the last tenants were pretty meticulous about how they left the place, but that didn't mean that they could not have forgotten a box or two in the basement. In fact, it was quite possible that in their rush to leave they had done just that. On the other hand, it was also possible that the boxes were the property of the people who lived here many years before. And that made Anthony wonder about something brand new. Who were the people that inhabited this house? Who lived here through the years? How many families had actually come to make this their home? And what might they have seen? All of it seemed to swirl in Anthony's head. He suddenly felt like a paleontologist discovering the remains of some long-forgotten dinosaur. He felt like the mysteries of this house were slowly beginning to reveal themselves to him in the form of his questions. He felt like asking a thousand of them. But right now he would content himself with just looking through some old boxes.

Anthony finished up two more boxes (old shoes and another Prince record, Controversy, was all he found) and then decided he should probably head upstairs. He pushed the boxes he had gone through to one side and headed for the stairs.

The kitchen was dark when he got up there. Only the light over the stove was on and the smell of baked chicken still lingered in the air from dinner. Had he really been down there that long? Had Jeanette and the kids ate dinner without him even knowing? And worst of all, why didn't anyone come down to check on him? He listened to see if anyone was still awake in the house but all was quiet. He thought it might have been too quiet. He opened the refrigerator and looked for something to nibble on. He hadn't realized how hungry he was until this very moment. Outside, the wind picked up and rattled the kitchen windows. Anthony turned from the fridge and looked outside. He could see the trees in the backyard swaying in the moonlight. He closed the fridge and went to the back door that led outside. He opened it and stepped outside.

The wind had grown stronger and he felt it whip across his face like a gentle slap. Off in the distance, the moonlight glistened off of the lake. Anthony inhaled the night air. He marveled at how clean it smelled out here away from the true suburbs and hustle and bustle of so much combustion. He took one last deep breath and then turned and went into the house. A strong wind blew through as he was closing the door.

Anthony headed for the stairs, and ultimately for his bed and some much needed rest. But if he had stayed in the kitchen he might have seen something come inside with him when he closed the kitchen door.

A wind swirled in the kitchen, gently ruffling some napkins on the kitchen table. The wind moved over the furniture and through the appliances until finally settling near the back door in a kind of funnel cloud. It whipped up its intensity and then dispersed like magic. The wind was gone, but in its place was a ghostly image of two children. Two children that looked like Michael and Taylor. And one was standing over the other with playing cards, smiling.

It took a moment for Anthony to realize that he was alone in his bed. He shook the sleep out of his head and looked over at the clock on the nightstand. It was flashing 12:00. He looked around the room for some sign of Jeanette, but everything was quiet. He also noticed the bedroom door was closed. He jumped out of bed and threw on his robe. He pulled the bedroom door open and immediately heard the voices of his children somewhere downstairs.

"Thank God," he said under his breath.

He made his way to the bathroom and took a piss. More laughter from downstairs and the sound of Jeanette telling Michael to behave himself at the table. He finished up in the bathroom and made his way downstairs.

The three of them were sitting at the kitchen table eating breakfast. He could not have been more relieved. They noticed him right away.

"Good morning, Daddy," Taylor said through a mouthful of Fruit Loops.

Anthony kissed her head and sat down next to Jeanette.

"I missed dinner last night. Why didn't you guys come and get me?" Anthony asked.

"Well, the kids were hungry and you seemed pretty preoccupied with that stuff in the basement."

"Yeah, I guess I was. I must have lost track of time. When I came up the whole house was quiet," he said.

"You have some explaining to do, sir," Jeanette said.

"Uh oh. What did I do now?" Anthony said.

"You left the back door wide open."

Anthony remembered going outside for a minute. But he also remembered shutting and locking that door.

"Really? Because I remember locking it."

"Did you go outside for something?" Jeanette asked.

"I did. When I came up stairs and saw that everyone had gone to bed, I went outside for a bit of fresh air. But I distinctly remember closing and locking that door. Was anything broken?"

"No. Everything seems to be in order. I just hate to think that anything or anyone could have just walked into our house in the middle of the night," Jeanette said.

"It's scary, Dad," Taylor said.

"Yeah. What if some creature from the lake strolled in here and drank my brains?" Michael said.

The whole table laughed at this and the mood instantly became lighter. Maybe he had forgotten to close that door after all, but he really didn't think so. He suddenly remembered the wind when he went outside last night and wondered if maybe it had blown the door open. But hadn't he locked it? He was sure he had. Oh well, he would have to be more careful next time. Right now he was just happy to be with his family.

"So two more weeks till school, right?" Jeanette said.

Both Taylor and Michael sighed in unison.

"Don't remind us," they said.

"Enjoy your last bits of freedom. Because when school starts you will both be relegated to the dark dungeon to do your homework," Anthony said, cackling in his best evil villain voice.

The kids rolled their eyes and grabbed their dishes from the table. They dumped them in the sink and took off into the living room. Now Anthony and Jeanette were alone at the table.

"So, here we are," Jeanette said.

"Yes. Just the two of us," Anthony said, raising his eyebrows at her.

"Oh, Mr. Morrison. You are an insatiable man! Do behave."

"You have a two week reprieve from my sexual advances. But once the kids go back to school, it's on," he said.

"Don't tease me," she said, biting her lip.

(12)

The end of summer came hard and fast. School began in earnest on August 21st. Anthony drove Taylor and Michael on the first day. They were a bit farther away from their school, but at least they didn't have to change schools. They would be able to finish out their middle school life with the same friends. Anthony and Jeanette agreed that this was best. So Anthony made sure everyone was up and ready on time. They hopped in the car and headed off for school. Jeanette kissed the three of them and then watched them drive off.

She was amazed at how quickly her babies were growing up. One minute they were hanging off of her breasts and the next they were studying for a pre-algebra exam. Life was a series of wonderful joys and sinister cruelties. The joys were obvious. You give birth to something so wonderful and beautiful. And then you watch them grow right before your eyes, but never fully enjoying the time you have because you're so worried about taking care of them. And then, suddenly, they're grown up. Poof! Just like magic. But Jeanette was not one to dwell on it. She was blessed in so many ways. She had a wonderful husband who took pride in taking care of his family. They all had their health. And at the end of the day, they were doing just fine. Jeanette smiled at this thought. She knew she had nothing to be sad about.

She pulled the sweater she was wearing tight around her chest as a chilly wind whipped across the porch.

"Damn," she said aloud. Behind her she heard the front door slam shut. She turned quickly at the sound, startled. She opened the door and went inside as another gust of wind blew through the front door. She pushed it closed and locked it. That's when she heard the sound of laughter from upstairs.

"Oh my God." It escaped her lips without her even knowing she had said it. But she was genuinely spooked right now. Why was there laughter coming from upstairs? A thousand thoughts raced through her mind. And then it hit her. Taylor had left her TV on. That's what it was. She started to make her way upstairs when the laughter suddenly stopped. She stopped midway up the stairs and heard them creak under her feet. A moment of silence and then laughter again. Jeanette took the rest of the stairs at a run and went into Taylor's room.

The TV was on. It was a commercial for something or other. Jeanette laughed out loud and shut it off. "Going a little nutty," she said. She straightened up Taylor's bed and left the room. She had just made it to the top of the stairs when the laughter started again.

"Son of a bitch!" she said.

This time the sound was coming from her own bedroom. She was sure of it. She turned around and went into her bedroom. The windows were open and a strong wind was blowing through. She made her way to the window and looked out. Far out, across the lake she could see boaters and people skiing. There was the faint echo of laughter and the sound of an Outboard motor scrambling along.

"Starting to lose your mind, old girl," Jeanette said. She pulled the window closed and tidied up the curtains. She turned around and was frozen by what she saw on the bed.

She would later be amazed at how little fear she initially felt when she saw what she saw. It was only later, after everything had settled down that Jeanette got a cold chill up her spine and the hair on her arms stood up at the very thought of it. But right now, standing in front of her bed, there was only a rising anger.

The image was very much like a ghost. It was cloudy and dreamy and seemed to go out of focus every few seconds. But it stayed centered on the bed. What Jeanette saw in the ghostly image was Anthony. And he was on top of another woman. Jeanette was not sure who the woman was: She had never seen her before. Anthony was moving his hips back and forth, stopping only once in his rhythm to lean down and kiss the woman on the neck. There was no noise coming from the bed. Jeanette put her hand to her mouth and startled herself by letting out a small cry.

"This is crazy," she said aloud, unable to take her eyes from the ghost. And then another gust of wind blasted through the room and the image swirled away into nothing. Jeanette turned around to make sure the window was closed. It was. So where did that gust of wind just come from, she wondered. And now, only after everything had settled to a whisper, did the first prick of fear creep into her. She shivered and ran from the room. She ran downstairs and pulled open the front door. Seconds later she was standing in the front yard holding her arms tight against her sides and shaking.

Jeanette was debating whether she should call Anthony right now. She wanted to. She wanted to call him and demand he explain to her why she saw him on top of another woman. But then she realized that that would sound ludicrous. What she SAW was not Anthony at all, but an image of Anthony. What she saw was a ghost. So the most important thing was the ghost, wasn't it? And yet the only thing she kept running through her mind was that her husband was cheating on her. He was seeing some tramp and was sleeping with her on a regular basis. He probably put her up in some apartment nearby so that he could have her whenever the urge struck him. Bastard!

"This is crazy," Jeanette said aloud to the empty kitchen. She had been sitting at the table sipping on coffee for close to an hour. She kept playing the scene out in her head. She remembered closing the curtains in the bedroom and then turning around to see the image on the bed. She remembered how Anthony leaned in and kissed the woman on her neck. She slammed her fist down on the table and her coffee sloshed out.

"This is crazy," she said again.

She decided she would call him. So she grabbed the phone from the charger and dialed him at work. He picked it up on the first ring.

"Hello?" he said.

"Anthony? It's me. Listen, something just happened in the house and I really need to talk to you about it."

"What happened? Are you all right?"

"Oh, I'm fine. But I saw something that was a bit off," she said.

"What was it?" he asked.

"It can wait til you get home."

"What was it, sweetie?" he pressed.

"I said it could wait!" She hung the phone up, immediately regretting how she had just spoken to him. After all, he had not done anything wrong. It was only a strange ghostly image that just happened to appear on her bed in the middle of the morning. Nothing odd about that. Jeanette smiled for the first time in almost an hour and got up. She would talk to him when he got home. And they would talk about it like adults. She made a promise to herself that she would stay calm. If nothing else, she would stay calm.

(13)

Anthony sat looking at the phone for a moment before he clicked it off. He was not quite sure why his wife just snapped at him, but it bothered him. He set the phone on his desk and looked up to see Peter Siegelman standing in the doorway. He was leaning against the frame and smirking.

"Family problems?" Peter asked.

"Excuse me?" Anthony said.

"I couldn't help but overhear your conversation," he said.

"You know, I can't remember seeing you in my office more than maybe five times since you started. And now, in the past month, I think I've seen you something like five times. Its way too much, Peter." Anthony hoped his sarcasm was not lost on the man. Anthony knew that this was not the time to be dealing with this idiot, but why was he here.

"Is there something I can do for you?" Anthony asked.

"Yeah, I was hoping you could tell me what's going on at your new house. Rumor has it the place is haunted. Something about slavery, I think."

"You really come across as a bit of a prick, you know that?" Anthony regretted it the moment it left his lips. But between his wife hanging up on him and this guy standing in his office asking about his personal business, Anthony had had enough. So he let loose into Peter Siegelman and hoped that his message would be loud and clear.

"A prick, huh?" Peter said.

"How many times have you seen me in your office, Peter? Never. I don't come down there because I have no business down there. But also because I have nothing to say to you. I don't know where you live or the history of your home. And I also don't give a shit. So why would you take so much valuable time from your day to come up and ask me about my home?"

"So is the place haunted?" Peter said, still smirking.

"Do you think it's haunted? Have you heard that it's haunted?" Anthony asked.

"I heard some things, yeah. And none of them were good. I also heard that your neighbor likes to eat children."

"So if you heard these things, then they must be true, right? I mean surely wherever you heard them was a reliable source. And why am I having this conversation with you?" Anthony stood up, walked around his desk and pushed Peter from the room. He slammed his office door closed and leaned against it. He exhaled deeply and tried to remember the last time he felt so stressed out. He wanted to leave for the day. The kids would be in school for another four hours. He could go home, check on Jeanette and sort that problem out and then he could pick up Taylor and Michael from school. He went back to his desk to grab his things when the phone rang.

"What now?" he said aloud, picking up the phone and answering it.

"Mr. Morrison?" the voice asked.

"Yes."

"This is Sandy Duncan at St Patrick's. We've had an incident with your son Michael at school today."

Anthony leaned his head in his free hand and closed his eyes. Could this day possibly get any worse? He breathed deep and then opened his eyes. He tried to calm himself before he went on with the phone call.

"What happened?" he asked.

"Well, it's probably best if you come down to the school. Either you or Mrs. Morrison."

"No. I'll be there shortly. Thank you." Anthony hung up the phone and sat for only a moment before gathering up his things and storming from his office. He had no idea that as bad as things seemed right now, they were only going to get worse.

(14)

The drive to the school was horrible. He kept tossing around the idea that he should call Jeanette and tell her about Michael. But then he remembered how she snapped at him on the phone and had no desire to deal with any of that right now. Anthony thought how as recently as yesterday all things seemed to be normal. And then in one short afternoon, his whole world seemed to be tilting. He felt like he was on the deck of some capsizing ship, hanging on to anything as his feet slid on the slippery deck. It was maddening. And then his thoughts turned to his son. What could he have done to get himself in trouble? Had he gotten into a fight? Was it something he said? Anthony punched the steering wheel.

"Dammit!" he said out loud, turning the wheel to pull into the school's parking lot. He killed the engine and got out. School was still in session, so the parking lot was quiet. Anthony slid between cars and weaved his way to the front office.

Michael was sitting just to the right of the door when Anthony walked in. He gave his dad a reproachful look and then looked down at his hands. Anthony walked past him, slapping him gently in the head. He slid up to the desk that seemed to take up the entire wall and asked to see the principal.

"Ms. Duncan will be right out, sir. If you'd like to take a seat, I'll call you when she's done," said the receptionist.

"Thank you," Anthony said and then turned towards Michael and sat down next to him. "What did you do?" he asked.

"Dad, please," Michael said.

Anthony gave him a look that seemed to suggest anger and Michael said no more. A moment later Sandy Duncan, the principal, came out of her office and called Anthony and Michael back. They both got up, Michael leading the way to the office. Anthony noticed another boy sitting in a chair inside of Sandy's office. He looked like he had been crying. Anthony sat down next to Michael in another chair and waited for the bad news. Sandy Duncan wasted no time getting down to it.

"Mr. Morrison, thank you for coming so quickly. I'd like to fill you in on what happened today and then we can go from there, okay?"

"Great," Anthony said.

"Okay, well, it started like this."

(15)

Anthony pulled onto the gravel driveway and put the car in park. He looked over at Michael and stared at him. In the backseat, Taylor said nothing. They sat that way for several minutes before Taylor finally chimed in from the back.

"Can I go in the house?"

Anthony seemed to snap out of his thoughts. He looked back at Taylor and nodded. "Tell mom we'll be right in. I want to talk to Michael for a second."

Michael exhaled and rolled his eyes. He knew he was about to get lectured. And in Michael's young mind and limited experience, there was nothing worse than being lectured. But he was also old enough, and smart enough, to know that he probably had it coming. What he did in school was less than smart. So he rolled down his window and braced himself for the talk.

Anthony turned off the engine and rolled down his own window. He hung his arm out, feeling the gentle breeze that was swirling outside. He marveled at how beautiful the weather was this time of the year. The trees had begun to change, and they were a beautiful scarlet and gold. And the weather was still just crisp enough not to need a jacket. Winter was just around the corner and Anthony had an idea that it would be beautiful. He imagined snow-covered trees and the lake in back of the house iced over. He saw himself sledding with his kids and even making snowmen in the front yard. It felt like something out of a painting. He smiled and then shook himself back to reality.

"So?" Michael said.

"I know the last thing in the world you want to hear right now is a lecture," Anthony started. He could see relief spill out all over his son's face. "But I do need to make it clear that this can not happen ever again. Is that clear?"

Michael nodded.

"I need to know you understand, Michael."

"I do understand, Dad. It was a dumb mistake. I know that. And I am sorry."

"Okay. But I do have a question," Anthony said.

"Okay."

"At what point did you feel like fighting with this other boy?"

"What do you mean?" Michael asked.

"I mean, at what point did the situation go from an argument to a physical fight?"

Michael looked down at his hands and Anthony noticed how thoughtful he looked at that moment. He couldn't remember ever seeing his son this sad before. And suddenly his heart ached. He wanted to reach across the seat and give his son a great big hug. But he also knew that part of the learning process came from the pain that we endure when we do something wrong. It's how we learn, Anthony knew. So he held back on the hug and instead just waited for Michael to answer.

Finally, Michael looked up from his hands and turned his gaze on Anthony. "It was when he called me a nigger," Michael said, and then he broke down in tears.

Anthony let him cry for only a few seconds before reaching across the seat and giving his son a hug. He squeezed him tight and didn't let him go until he felt the sobs subside to mere sniffles. He could only hope that he had exorcised the pain in his son's heart. But he had a sneaking suspicion that this was only the beginning.

They sat in the car for a few more minutes until Michael could compose himself. Then, with two huge sighs, they both got out and headed into the house. Anthony was dreading what might be waiting for him inside. He knew he would have to deal with Jeanette at some point, but he really wasn't up for it. The day had taken its toll on him and he really wanted nothing more than to go inside and have a beer. Something cold and frothy and strong enough to calm his nerves. He watched Michael slide in the front door and then followed him in. At his back, a strong wind whirled around and then slid into the house behind him.

Jeanette was waiting for him when he walked in. Anthony was sure that the look on her face was a frown. But after a moment he realized that his mind was playing tricks on him. She was really smiling. He smiled back at her and gave her a big hug.

"Is everything okay?" Anthony asked.

"Yes," she said.

Anthony left it at that. He knew they would have time to talk later, when the kids were in bed and the house was quiet. He could only hope she wasn't lying, and everything was truly okay. He would find out. Taylor ran into the front hallway where they were standing. She looked upset. Anthony pulled away from Jeanette and grabbed Taylor's shoulders.

"What is it, sweetie?' Anthony asked.

"It's Michael. He just saw something."

"What do you mean?" Jeanette asked.

"I don't know, but it's not good," Taylor said.

The three of them ran from the room and into the kitchen where Michael was curled up against the black glass of the oven. He was trembling.

Anthony and Jeanette ran over to him and squatted down. They both put their arms around him, feeling him shake against their hold. Something had frightened him to his core.

"Michael? What happened, baby?" Jeanette asked, stroking his head. But Michael only continued to shake. He kept shooting sharp glances towards the far corner of the kitchen. Anthony followed his son's eyes and that's when he saw it. It was hovering near the kitchen table.

Anthony felt goose bumps when he saw it. It seemed like a very vague ghostly image of a woman holding a baby. She was rocking the baby in her arms and was singing. Jeanette noticed him staring and turned her own eyes towards the other side of the kitchen. She jumped slightly when she saw it. Anthony looked down at Michael and then stood up. He noticed Taylor standing in the doorway to the living room.

"Stay there, Taylor," Anthony said, moving towards the shadowy image hovering in his kitchen. Anthony moved slowly towards the image. When he got close to it, the ghostly woman looked up from her baby and stared at Anthony. He felt a horrible chill rip through his body and settle on his brain. He suddenly felt so *cold*. The woman put one long finger to her lips. She was telling Anthony to be quiet. He stopped where he was and held out his hand towards the woman. His hand passed through her image only slightly breaking the continuity of her form. She continued to hold her finger to her lips. And then, inexplicably, she spoke.

"The baby is sleeping," she said.

Anthony was startled out of his stance and nearly fell backwards. He steadied himself and approached the woman again. She held a hand out to him suggesting that he stop. He did. And then she pulled the blanket that the baby was wrapped in over the child's head, covering its face.

"I won't let her get my baby. I won't," the woman said.

Anthony felt that coldness wrap him up again. He shivered slightly and continued to simply stare in awe at the sight before him. Jeanette had moved behind him and put a hand on his shoulder. He jumped when she touched him. "Dammit! Don't do that. You scared the crap out of me!"

Jeanette pulled him close and hugged him. They both looked on at the woman. Off in the corner of the kitchen, Michael continued to shake. He couldn't believe what he was seeing. To his eyes, it was more than just a woman holding a baby. To him it meant that something terrible was living in his house. And that terrible thing was watching them. He couldn't understand why his mother and father would want to even be near that thing. But there they were, standing right next to it, attempting to touch it.

He pushed himself up against the wall as hard as he could, hoping that he could just disappear into the wall itself. But it remained firm against his back so he just closed his eyes. He had no desire to watch anything else.

The ghostly woman suddenly looked scared. She pulled her baby tight against her chest and looked around wildly. Anthony tried to follow her gaze, looking around the kitchen for what she might be seeing. And then, inexplicably, the woman vanished in a swirl of faint smoke. Anthony stood still, Jeanette holding him tighter than before.

No one said anything for several minutes. Anthony looked from his wife to Michael, still against the wall, and finally to Taylor standing around the corner of the kitchen doorway, peeking in. He pulled himself loose from Jeanette and walked over to Michael. His son looked up at him, tears streaming down his face. The horror they had all experienced had been real. And Anthony had an idea that things were probably going to get much worse.

(16)

"Well, we can't stay here," Michael said. He was curled up on the couch with a big brown comforter pulled tight over his shoulders. Anthony was sitting next to him. Jeanette and Taylor were huddled together on the love seat.

"I agree," Taylor said.

"Listen, I know we've all just had a very real scare tonight. And for the record, I'm scared too. But we need to calm down and talk about this," Anthony said.

"Dad, there's something wrong here. Why are we even discussing this?" Michael was agitated and shoved the comforter off of his shoulders in a huff. Anthony put a hand on his shoulder and held him with a firm grip.

"Calm," Anthony said. "We're going to talk about it because that's what we should do. I've never given a single thought to ghosts my entire adult life. But now, after what we saw in the kitchen, I'm forced to do just that. And knowing me as you all do, you know that I'm all about rationalizing. I'm all about talking about the problem and finding a solution. Whatever happened here tonight happened for a reason. That woman in the kitchen was scared. She was afraid that someone was coming for her baby. And why is that? I want to know." He let go of Michael's shoulder and leaned back on the couch. Michael seemed to relax as well.

"I saw something this morning," Jeanette said. She only now realized that she never had an opportunity to mention it earlier.

That the moment Anthony got home with the kids was when all hell broke loose. She sat silent for a moment and weighed her words. She wanted to be clear about what she saw. She also wanted to be careful not to say anything inappropriate in front of her kids. She remembered a time when Taylor was just learning how to talk. Jeanette had been on the phone with her mother when she said shit a little too loud and Taylor spent the rest of the day running around the house in her diapers, rattling the word shit with perfect clarity. The memory made Jeanette smile a little. But then the memory of her husband on top of the other woman stole that smile away as quickly as it had come. Jeanette looked down at her hands and then up again at her family. They were all staring at her, waiting for her to tell her tale. She thought about forgetting the whole thing. Just tell them she was mistaken and they could go on having their family meeting about ghosts. But she also knew that somehow, the two stories were related. That the woman in the kitchen was the same woman she saw upstairs with her husband. Of that she was certain. Jeanette took a deep breath and began her tale.

"It was just after everyone left this morning. I heard a noise from upstairs and went up there to find Taylor's TV on." Jeanette glanced over at Taylor and saw a look on her face that suggested that she didn't remember leaving her TV on at all. She continued with the story. "So I shut the TV off and went into the hallway. Well, I heard the noise again, but this time from our bedroom. So I went in there and found the window open. I looked outside and saw some people out on the lake. I shut the window and turned around to find . . ." She choked up at this point and stifled some tears. It took her a moment to regroup and then she continued. "I saw you," she said, pointing at Anthony, "on the bed with another woman." That was it. She let loose an incredible sob and Anthony moved from his spot on the couch to her side on the love seat. He held her tight, squeezing her as mad sobs racked through her body. Taylor and Michael looked on intently.

Anthony turned to Michael and Taylor. "Go upstairs, please," he said.

Taylor and Michael shared a horrified look. "We're not going up there," they said.

"Turn on every light in the house if you have to, but please give your mother and I some time alone. Thank you."

Michael and Taylor both knew that there would be no point in arguing. They grabbed their respective blankets and proceeded up the stairs, doing exactly as their father had instructed and turned on every light they could.

Anthony heard a door close upstairs and knew that they were no longer listening. He turned back to his wife and kissed her forehead. Then he got into the loveseat next to her. Jeanette's tears had quieted and she seemed herself again. "What's going on here?" she asked.

"I don't know, sweetie," Anthony replied. And he truly did not know what was going on. He knew only what he had seen with his own eyes, in the kitchen. But what his wife had seen earlier was something else entirely. That was something that bothered him much more.

Jeanette was staring at his face. She was studying him, he knew. Studying him with those lawyers eyes, looking for something that might give away if he was lying or not. And he was more than relieved when she dropped her gaze back to the floor.

"Anthony, I'm not sure if I can stay here any longer."

"What do you mean? This is our home."

"Oh come on. Are you so naïve to think that this is just some freak occurrence that won't happen again? There is something wrong with this house, and you know it. Hell, we knew it before we bought the place. But we were all so wrapped up in it that we thought nothing like this could ever happen to us." Jeanette was getting worked up now. She had thrown off her blanket and was now standing, pacing in front of Anthony.

"I get the impression that you blame me for all of this," Anthony said.

"Well, let's be honest. You did keep a lot of what you knew a secret from us. From your kids."

"I didn't think it was helpful telling my children about why the previous owners left this house."

"And how about now? Do you think it would be appropriate now? Is there anything else you're not telling me?" She hit him with a vicious look and he cringed as if she had slapped him.

"Are you suggesting that . . . that maybe what you saw upstairs was real somehow?" Anthony asked.

"I'm not suggesting anything. I only know what I saw. Now tell me what you would think?" she said.

"I would think that I saw a ghost, nothing more." He said.

"And maybe that's true, but what if those ghosts were the truth?"

"I don't follow you," he said.

"The woman in the kitchen was scared, right? You said yourself that you wanted to know what she was afraid of. Well, the woman in the kitchen was also the woman that you were with on our bed."

Anthony felt so cold. It was all hitting him now. And the chill that raced through his blood felt like ice. He was staring up at his wife, watching her lips move but no longer hearing the words. He was suddenly afraid of what all of this might mean. He was afraid of losing his family. And when he finally came back to his place on the loveseat, Jeanette was no longer speaking. She was grabbing her shoes from the near the front door and was putting them on.

"Wait. What are you doing?" Anthony asked.

"I told you, I'm not staying here. I'm taking the kids to a hotel until I can figure things out."

"What is there to figure out? We'll get to the bottom of this, I promise," he said.

"There is nothing to figure out, Anthony. There is something bad in this house and I am not going to let my kids be subjected to that. I mean, look at you. You're so desperate right now."

"What does that mean?" he asked.

"It means that you're on the verge of losing all that you love and you're still willing to stay here and figure it out."

"Oh, so you're leaving me unless I leave this house. Is that it?"

"We're not staying here. This conversation is over." Jeanette ran up the stairs and grabbed the kids. The three of them came down the stairs and moved out the front door. Anthony only stood there, watching them leave, never once thinking about stopping them. And for the life of him, he could not figure out why. Michael looked back only once as he was being rushed out the door and Anthony saw that he was crying again. Taylor looked back and blew her father a kiss.

Anthony closed his eyes and heard the front door slam shut. He let the room fall silent, the distant echo of the slamming door fading into the walls. He continued standing there, eyes closed, and let the quiet settle over him. He had so much to understand. Not the least of which was why he had just let his family walk out on him and he hadn't even put up a fight. His wife was right about one thing; he was desperate. But it was answers he wanted more than anything else. And he had an idea where he should start looking for them.

Outside, the wind had settled down and a light rain was starting to fall. It tapped against the windows, beating a steady thump that sounded like small fingers tapping at glass. Small fingers that just might be trying to get in.

(17)

Anthony stood in the basement staring at all of the crap around his feet. He had pulled open every box he found and had their contents strewn all over. He couldn't remember the last time he had eaten and a horrible rumbling ripped through his stomach. He growled out loud and headed upstairs to make a sandwich. When he was done, he grabbed a Coke from the pantry and went back downstairs. The boxes and their contents were still waiting for him.

The first thing he would do was to get his own stuff separated from the stuff from the other families. His own junk made up most of what was down here, but he there was still a sizable pile of foreign material. He only hoped it held some answers. He wanted to know why that woman seemed so scared and, he supposed, why he was making love to her. That part not only intrigued him, but made him shiver as well. Why would his wife see something like that? Was she even telling the truth? He caught himself feeling a tinge of anger towards her for the first time since he had met her. They fell in love almost at first sight, and Anthony had never felt anything but love and admiration for that woman. So why now, when things had suddenly gotten so bad in his life, was he feeling so angry towards her? Was it because she had taken the kids and walked out the door? Or maybe it was because he had done nothing to stop them. He had let them go without any sort of a fight. And with that, he decided he was probably angrier with himself.

He kicked the nearest box and cursed himself for even thinking like this. He had work to do. If he wanted to get back to his family, and get them back, he would need to find those elusive answers. He started with the box he had just kicked.

There was a stack of old papers in the box. Most of them were yellowed and frayed, but a few near the bottom of the box seemed in fine condition. He pulled those out and sat down on the cold concrete floor and began reading.

The first sheet he read had rows and columns with numbers. It looked like a spreadsheet with the information handwritten. Very few words were on it, but the one that caught his eye was handwritten across the upper right corner of the sheet. It looked like a child's handwriting, all scribbled and messy. But he could make it out. It said: Chains. That was odd. Just that single word, scrawled amid numbers that seemed to have no meaning to him. At the top of each column was a date. No years, just months and days. And from right to left it started with March and ended with November. Anthony had been around enough bankers and loan guys to know that no financial year ever started in March, and it most certainly did not end in November. So whatever these numbers represented, it was not finances. And yet every row had a dollar sign in front of it. Strange. He set that sheet aside, in a pile he began for stuff he wanted to keep. This would be the first of many.

The next paper that caught his attention was a formal letter, stamped with a seal that looked like an official state seal. There was no writing on the stamp, only the symbol of a goat. The letter itself was dated 14 February, 1969. The letterhead stated that it came from the office of Casale and Elliott, ASC. Anthony had always been a fan of the movies. He grew up watching them with his father and later on in life developed his own passion for the classics. So when he saw the letterhead and the ASC, he immediately thought of the union of cinematographers, American Society of Cinematographers, and wondered why that was even on this paper. And then he realized that it was entirely possible that was not what it meant at all. It could mean anything. Just because he thought it meant that certainly did not make it so. He put all thoughts about movies and unions aside and read the letter.

Dear Sir,

I am writing this letter to you today in the hopes that we can come to some sort of arrangement regarding our finances on the house. As we both know, our estate is indebted to your company in the amount of $240,000. My partner and I do not have the means to pay off that loan in full, but we would be willing to work out a payment plan that would be mutually agreeable. And while we both know that you are not obligated to give us any favors, we would truly be in your debt (no pun intended) if you could arrange something for us. And if by some chance you do not want to extend us some time in paying you back, there is another matter that we would be forced to indulge in. We are not ones to post threats, and this is certainly not a threat. But we would be remiss if we did not protect our assets. We look forward to hearing from you.

Yours truly,

Aaron Casale and Timothy Elliott

Anthony stared at the letter and smiled. This bit of juicy gossip intrigued him. He had no idea who this letter was written to or even if it was ever sent, but the thought that these guys, Casale and Elliott, would resort to something ugly suggested that there might be more to this story than what was on the surface. Anthony put the letter on his keep pile and found another sheet. This one was what appeared to be a child's drawing. There were stick figures along the bottom of the page and a giant yellow sun near the upper left corner. The figures had their arms raised up towards that bright yellow sun and something that resembled a dog was barking. A bubble over one of the sticks figures had some words in it. It said: I wish mommy would stop crying. Anthony felt a chill when he read that. What had the child that drew this picture seen? And what was making mommy cry? He looked at it only a moment longer before setting it on his keep pile and moved on to the next stack of papers.

He was there for hours, separating his papers. Finally, when his back ached from sitting in the same position for so long, he stood up and stretched. He could hear his back sigh with disagreement and knew that not even a good nights rest would prevent him from aching all day tomorrow. He looked down at his work and smiled. He felt good about what he was doing. He felt like maybe he could actually figure this thing out. Anthony turned out the lights and went upstairs to the kitchen.

The phone rang and Anthony looked at the clock on the stove. It was almost 3 in the morning. Who could be calling him? He grabbed the phone and clicked it on.

"Hello?" he said.

"Anthony? It's Jeanette. Were you sleeping?" she asked.

"Yes," he lied.

"Sorry. I just needed to talk to you," she said.

"You left me, Jeanette. You took my kids and left me."

"Anthony, I'm not calling to argue. I just need you to understand why," she said.

"I know, you think that it might be dangerous to stay here, right?" he said.

"Why do people stay in haunted houses, Anthony?" she asked.

"I give up. Why do they?" He was irritated now. Her questions seemed pointless.

"No. I'm asking you. Why do they? I could never figure it out. Your house is haunted, you get out. End of story. But you seem to be driven to find out *why* your house is haunted. Even at the expense of your family. Why?"

"Did you see the woman in our kitchen tonight, Jeanette? Did you see how frightened she was? I want to know what she was afraid of," he said.

"But why? She's not real. She was a goddamn ghost, Anthony! Whatever was chasing her was no longer around."

"And how do you know that? How do you know that whatever force was scaring her wasn't really in the house with her?"

"Okay, suppose it was, Anthony. Do you see where it might be a problem to be in that house anymore? Do you see how you have just proven my point?"

But he didn't. All he could think about now was how scared that woman looked. She was afraid of something. Something that may very well be living right here in this room. But he didn't care. He wanted answers more than anything. He wanted to save that woman. To make her feel safe with her child. But he never once thought about the safety of his own kids in this house. He hung up the phone and went to bed. There were no dreams that night. Only the soft patter of the raindrops on his window. And the gentle wind blowing all around the house. Swirling like a silk scarf caught in a breeze, flapping and moving like some organic dream.

(18)

Anthony heard the pounding on the front door. It was a persistent thud that didn't seem to stop. Was the doorbell not working, he thought. Was someone so eager to get his attention that they would pound on the door like that? Anthony pulled the down comforter off his body and loped out of bed. He went downstairs in his boxers and pulled the door open. Harriet Cray was standing on his porch, arm raised, ready to keep knocking if he had not answered. She looked wild-eyed and insane. A shock of white hair loose on the side of her normally well-kept head.

"Mrs. Cray. Can I help you?" Anthony said.

She returned her gaze to his eyes. "I'm sorry to wake you so early, but we have a little problem."

"And what might that be?" he said.

"Well, I'm not quite sure how to say this, but there's a woman at my house who says she needs to talk to you."

"A woman? My wife?" he asked, his mind a frenzy of thoughts still clouded by being woken up so early.

"Your wife? Isn't your wife here with you?" Harriet smirked, peeking her head around Anthony, trying to look into the house.

"Never mind. Who is it?" Anthony said.

"Well, I'm not sure. But she's very cute. And she's got a child with her."

Anthony went cold all over. He shuddered, thinking only of the woman in his kitchen the night before. The woman that he had slept with him in some ghostly sex act performed in front of his wife. A sex act he didn't see but could very well visualize.

"Did you hear me?" Harriet asked.

"Yes. I did. Let me get dressed and then I'll be right over."

Harriet had turned her back and was starting down the path towards the sidewalk when Anthony called after her.

"Did she ask for me specifically?" he asked.

Harriet paused and then turned to face Anthony. "She asked for the man living in this house." Harriet turned and continued walking. Anthony stood in the doorway only a moment longer. He was more confused than ever. But he was also intrigued. He thought he might finally be getting some answers. And yet it never occurred to him to ask why any of this was happening. All he cared about was getting some answers. And then maybe his wife and kids would come back to him. Come back to their house. And they could be a family once again.

He was dressed and out the door minutes later. It was chilly outside and a cold breeze covered his face as he walked. He noticed the trees along the sidewalk changing colors. Some even devoid of leaves altogether. It looked like winter. It had that cold feeling. Not the just the weather, but the feeling when everything around him was dying. That's what happened in the winter. The cold air killed the flowers and the leaves and left skeleton trees to watch over everything. He walked underneath those trees and thought of his own life. How had he gotten here? At what point did all that he love become second to finding answers. He didn't know. He couldn't remember crossing any kind of moral line in his head. But he had done it regardless. He had become the thing he swore he would never become.

The sidewalk grew darker as he got closer to the Cray house. The trees here were thicker and sturdier, holding up to the winter chill far better than the trees closer to his property. He moved through the shadows and made his way up to the front door of the Cray house. He barely had a chance to knock before Harriet had opened the door and welcomed him inside. He inhaled deeply, knowing only that he didn't know anything about anything. And that in itself was a bit comforting. Strange, but comforting.

It was warm inside. And that wonderful smell of baked apples hit him again. He smiled, knowing how good that smell made him feel. But his thoughts quickly came back to reality when he saw the woman standing next to Harriet. It was the woman from his kitchen, no doubt. But she seemed real, not some ghostly image like what he saw in his kitchen. She was holding a child, wrapped up warm in a blanket, just like before. She was trying to make eye contact with him, but kept looking down at the floor. Harriet motioned for everyone to come into the living room and sit down.

"I think I'll leave you two alone," Harriet said. She fluffed up some pillows on the couch and left the room.

"I guess I should ask who you are," Anthony said.

The woman managed to keep eye contact with Anthony, looking scared but eager to talk. She obviously had something to say. "My name is Maria, and this is my child Isabella. I know you don't know us. And it must be strange that I asked for you to come here. But I needed to talk to you."

Anthony leaned forward on the couch. He was suddenly thrilled at the thought of getting some answers. All those hours spent in the basement, digging through all sorts of old junk that may not even be relevant, and all he got was more questions. But now, sitting across from this strange woman, was he thinking that maybe all things would be revealed. Or maybe not.

"It's strange. But to be honest, not nearly as strange as you think. My name is Anthony. Or did you already know that?" he said.

"I didn't know your name until Mrs. Cray told me. All I knew was where you lived and that I had to talk to you."

"Why didn't you come to my house?" he asked.

"I knew you had a wife, and I didn't want to cause any problems. I thought this might be more appropriate. I hope you understand," she said, pulling the blanket from her child's face. She adjusted the child in her arms and settled back in the couch.

"Well, I don't understand at all, actually. But I think we could probably figure things out."

"You talk like a lawyer," she said.

"My wife was a lawyer many years ago. Maybe she rubbed off on me." They both shared a small laugh. Anthony felt the mood in the room lighten just a bit.

"Yes, maybe. I do have one favor to ask, though," Maria said.

"Sure," Anthony said.

"Just listen to what I have to say before asking me any questions. It's hard enough telling this to a stranger. I hope you understand."

Anthony nodded. "Of course," he said.

Maria took a deep breath and then began her tale.

"I feel like what I have to say is important because it concerns me, but I also know in the big scheme of things this may not seem so important. I'm a simple woman; it's just me and Isabella. But we make due the best we can. I live a short ride from here, in an apartment paid for by a man named Holden Elliott."

Anthony's ears perked up. Where had he heard that name before? Maria continued.

" He takes care of me. It's nothing sexual, just a simple arrangement between him and the father of Isabella. I'm only twenty-two but I tend to be mature for my age; at least that's what Holden says. Anyway, my problems started when the last tenants of your house were living there. I met that family through Holden and he arranged for me to stay there for a few days. They had children and he thought it would be good for me to be with other adults. And I liked it there. They were very kind to Isabella and I. But then, suddenly, the wife became very angry with me. She accused me of trying to sleep with her husband. I kept to myself when the kids went to bed, so I'm not sure why she thought that. But whatever it was made her mad. She asked me to leave the house and to never come back. I told Holden all about it and he did nothing. He said I was just being paranoid. But I'm sure of what happened.

I spent the next couple of weeks back at my apartment. But one day I got a phone call from a Richard LeBrock. He was the man in charge of selling the property that you now live in. He asked if I knew anything about the family that lived there. He said that they left rather suddenly and wanted to know what happened. I had no answers, obviously, but I was still a bit sad. I felt like I had caused this somehow. Like I had made them unhappy to live there."

Maria fell silent for a moment and Anthony could feel the air in the room suddenly get much heavier again. He had no jokes to lighten the mood, so he only continued to listen, hoping that this strange woman's story would become coherent. He was lost. There seemed to be no connecting thread to him at all. Where did he fit in this picture? He bit his tongue, knowing that he would have plenty of questions when Maria was finished.

"So I told Mr. LeBrock about what I thought might have happened," Maria continued. "He told me not to worry about it. Holden said the same thing. So I didn't, until you moved in the house."

Harriet came back into the room just then carrying a large serving tray with a pot of steaming tea and three cups on it. She set the tray on the coffee table in front of Anthony and Maria and started serving the tea. Anthony accepted his but Maria declined, choosing instead to rock her baby more forcefully.

Anthony took note of how nervous she had suddenly become when Harriet came into the room. She seemed to be holding her baby tighter than before, and a small film of perspiration had formed on her forehead. The smell of baked apples had subsided and gave way to the smell of another pleasant spice. Anthony inhaled deeply, sipping on tea and taking in the scene playing out in front of him. He couldn't remember a time in his life when he felt so confused. And so completely out of control. He wanted to ask Maria so many questions, but he wasn't sure if she was even done talking. So he simply waited.

Harriet sat down next to Maria and put her hand on the young girls knee. Maria didn't seem to notice. She just continued to rock Isabella. Finally, Maria looked up at Anthony and continued her story.

" To put it simply, Mr. Morrison, there is something living in your house."

That was all she said, but it was enough to send a violent shiver ripping through Anthony's spine. He twisted where he sat, trying his best to stay focused. But what she said had really bothered him. He knew something was there, he saw it not too long ago. And what he saw in his kitchen looked eerily similar to the woman that sat across from him right now. So that wasn't the problem. It was hearing it come out of someone else's mouth that bothered him. It gave it weight somehow. Made it real. He thought of his wife and kids sitting in some hotel room somewhere, lamenting their father's lack of compassion. He suddenly wanted to be with them very badly. Jeanette had been right; he was desperate.

"I beg your pardon?" Anthony said.

"You heard me right. And I also know by your reaction that you've felt it. Maybe you've even seen it," Maria said.

"What exactly have I seen, Maria?"

"Holden called it the truth," Maria said.

Anthony wanted to scream. He had no idea what this woman was talking about. He took a deep breath, weighing his words carefully. He wanted to be clear, but he did not want to sound desperate. He thought of Jeanette again. His heart was starting to ache for her. And for his children.

"I don't understand why you've brought me here," Anthony said, directing the question more towards Harriet than Maria. Harriet seemed to perk up when he asked this, as if she was daydreaming.

"If you're asking me, Mr. Morrison," Harriet started. "You would do well to think carefully about the first time we met."

Anthony thought back to that first meeting in this very room. He remembered how it smelled, that same scent of the apples. But he also remembered a vague, queer feeling in the room. As if there was an undercurrent of filth sitting just below the pleasant veneer of Harriet Cray's rustic sensibilities. He did remember their first meeting. It was the reason why he kept Harriet Cray at a distance. She felt a little off.

"I remember it. You told me some things about my house."

"That's correct. And yet here you sit, looking shocked when this girl tells you that something may be living in your home. Something unexplainable. Why?" Harriet asked.

"I love the house. I was drawn to it, I suppose. I guess I also hoped that the stories I heard were nothing more than fairy tales," Anthony said.

"And now?" Maria asked.

"Well, now I'm not so sure about anything," Anthony said.

"Meaning?" Harriet said.

"Meaning that I am still at a loss to figure out why I am sitting here talking to you two," Anthony said.

Harriet suddenly stood up and straightened out her housedress. She cleared her throat with a loud harrumph and began cleaning up the cups from the table.

"My husband and son will be home soon. I will have to ask both of you to leave now."

Maria stood up and headed for the front door. Harriet picked up the serving tray and called out to Maria.

"We'll see you soon, sweetie," Harriet said.

Maria barely turned her head, instead continuing to move to the front door. She opened it and walked outside.

Anthony stood where he was for several seconds before shaking his own head and making for the front door. Harriet stood where she was, staring at Anthony.

"Thanks for coming, Mr. Morrison. I always enjoy our little chats."

"Thank you for having me. How is Maria getting home?" he asked.

"She'll find her way. She always does." Harriet said.

Anthony nodded and then made his way out the front door. A cold gust of wind greeted him. He scanned the front yard and saw that Maria was already gone. But where? And how? Anthony pulled his jacket tight around his chest and started his walk home. He had a million things to figure out. Not the least of which was how his life had suddenly gotten so completely out of whack. He stared at the sidewalk all the way home, counting each crack in the pavement, hoping they would reveal something. Instead, they only brought more questions. And questions without answers were maddening.

Anthony was almost to his front porch when he heard the children laughing. It was a high, shrill sound coming from behind his house. He paused on the sidewalk that ended at his front porch and listened intently. Another round of laughter, this time more muted somehow, like it was farther away. Anthony moved towards the side of the house and that's when he saw the horribly disfigured shape slink away behind the house.

He had only caught a glimpse of it, but he knew it was not normal. It was black, with long legs that seemed bent at awkward angles. And something like a hat was perched on its head. Anthony paused only a second and then sprinted around the corner. He was greeted with nothing but the cold air swirling through the backyard. There was no disfigured shape slithering around back here and Anthony actually felt relief.

"Getting jumpy, old man," Anthony said. A gentle breeze swirled around his head and then he heard the laughter again. This time it seemed to be coming from his own backyard, all around him. And there, sunk low against the far corner of the house, almost down to the ground, was that horrible face looking up at him. A terrible chill rippled across Anthony's entire body. He had never felt so cold and afraid. And yet he could not take his eyes from the thing that was staring back him from a distance. He looked closer and saw that it may have been a woman, black hat sitting crooked on her head, dark smudges under her eyes, staring back at him. He raced towards the face, eager to know what was happening, when the air suddenly turned icy cold and blasted through the backyard with such ferocity that Anthony actually stumbled as he made his way to the other end of the house. And finally, rounding the corner, only to see that there was nothing there at all. No hideous, disfigured woman staring back at him. No children laughing and playing. There was only the wind. Blowing.

(19)

Anthony slammed the front door behind him and threw his keys across the room.

"Dammit!" he screamed. He went into the kitchen and grabbed the phone from the charger. He dialed his wife's cell and waited for her to answer. Several rings later, and no answer, he waited for her message to play out and then left a message.

"Jeanette, it's me. I just wanted to see how you guys were doing. I don't even know where you are, but I miss the kids terribly. I want to see you. All of you. Please call me." He clicked the phone off and dropped it on the floor. Then he fell back against the wall and slid down, fresh tears erupting from his eyes.

None of it made any sense. In the matter of a few short months his whole life had spiraled out of control. And for the first time he made the connection to the house. This house. The house that he had fallen in love with from the moment he first laid eyes on it. The house that he brought his family into to sleep. All of his problems stemmed from that one thing. He slammed his fist into the wall behind him, cursing himself for not seeing it. He hated how low he fallen. He hated the man he had become just recently. And he hated himself for wanting to stay here, even after he knew he should just leave. Something was holding him in place, urging him to find the answers. But answers to what? That was the worst part, not knowing.

"FUCK!" Anthony screamed aloud, pounding at the wall again. "WHAT DO YOU WANT FROM ME?!"

He continued sobbing, holding his head in his hands, racking his brain for the answer that would not come.

The phone rang almost twenty minutes later. Anthony was still sitting on the floor when it did and he reached across the floor and grabbed the phone. He flipped it over in his hands and answered.

"Hello?"

"Anthony? It's me. Are you okay?"

"I miss my kids, Jeanette. I miss you," Anthony said.

"I know, Sweetie. We miss you too. Michael's worried about his Daddy."

Anthony pulled the phone away from his mouth as a fresh bout of tears exploded. He composed himself as best he could and then put the phone back to his ear. "I miss them so much."

"We need to talk. I'm going to get someone to watch Taylor and Michael and then I'm coming over. Give me a few hours."

"Okay," he said. He clicked the phone off and dropped it back on the floor.

Jeanette and the kids had only been gone for the better part of twenty-four hours, but it felt much longer than that. He felt like he hadn't seen them in almost a month. And now Jeanette was on her way over to talk. Anthony knew she would try to talk him into leaving the house. Just cut their losses and sell the place. And in the meantime live in some hotel while they figured it all out. But he didn't want to leave the house. The possibility of ghosts didn't bother him. But not learning the truth bothered him very much. It suddenly came to him where he might find some answers.

His boss, Jonah Castle, seemed very eager to tell him about the history of his place before he bought it, so maybe now he could shed some more light on it. And maybe that little prick Peter Siegelman in Layout might even prove to be useful. Anthony suddenly felt invigorated. He had a new goal and he felt closer to getting to the truth. But right now, Jeanette was on her way over to talk. He would have to keep her happy without giving in. He had no intention of leaving anytime soon.

Anthony pulled himself up from the floor and looked around. He straightened up the kitchen and made his bed. And then he simply waited on the couch. He wanted to be ready.

(20)

Jeanette was nervous. She pulled into the driveway and turned off the car. She felt disconnected somehow, like she was visiting the house of a friend and not her own home. But she also knew what she saw in her kitchen. That image of a horrified woman and her child, and the awful image of that same woman making love to her husband. Something like that made you feel less than comforted. So she sat for a moment and tried to remember what she liked about the house when she first saw it. She loved the look of it, obviously, but there was also a great charm here. The house had a weight to it that suggested happiness. You could feel it not only in the house but also in the yard all the way back to the lake. The trees seemed to sing and dance in the breeze and a picturesque sky completed the painting.

Jeanette smiled for the first time in nearly two days and got out of the car. She took a quick look around and then made her way towards the front door. Somewhere behind the house, in the lake maybe, a bird whooped. She climbed the three steps up the porch and opened the front door.

Anthony was sitting on the couch. His eyes were swollen and he looked as if he hadn't slept in days. Jeanette knew he had been crying. She could hear it on the phone, but she had no idea how miserable he looked. In all their years of marriage, and even when they were just dating, she never knew him to be down. He always saw the positive side of things and told her that the glass was always half full. But now, seeing him like this, she was reminded of why it was of the utmost importance to get him out of this house. Not only for their family but also for his own life as well. She had to save him from himself.

"You look nice," Anthony said, not getting up from his spot on the couch.

Jeanette pulled off her coat and threw it over the back of the love seat and then sat down next to Anthony. She grabbed his shoulders and pulled him close. She could feel his whole body tighten for a brief moment and then relax and fall into her. She hugged him long and hard, feeling sobs rack his body. She would let him cry first. There would be time to talk. But right now she knew he just had to purge. To get every bit of sadness and sorrow out of his body. To come clean.

Finally, Anthony pulled himself back and looked at his wife. He marveled at how beautiful she was. He always thought she was beautiful. But she seemed to be positively glowing right now. Like an angel. "You look so beautiful," he said.

"Thank you," Jeanette replied. "Can we talk?"

Anthony wiped tears from his face and sniffed. "Of course," he said.

"No. I mean really talk. No arguing. No yelling. Just the truth?" she said.

Anthony nodded. "Of course."

"Good. Anything you want to start with?" Jeanette asked.

Anthony paused, thinking about the last day's events. He knew he should probably tell Jeanette everything, so he started with Harriet Cray's knock on the front door this morning.

He gave her everything, watching her expression change throughout his story. He knew she would ask questions, but right now she only listened intently. He finished with his walk home and then waited for Jeanette to speak.

"Okay, that's really strange. But what happened with the young woman, Maria?" Jeanette asked.

"I don't know. By the time I got out of the house, she was nowhere in sight. Maybe that man was waiting for her, Holden."

"Yeah, maybe," Jeanette said, but she didn't like it. It was all too convenient. They get a visit from a ghost in their home and then the next morning a woman who bears a striking resemblance to that ghost wants to talk to her husband. A ghost that also appeared in her bed on top of a vision of her husband, no less.

"Did you ever wonder why Harriet is so involved in all of this? I mean she seems to have her finger on the pulse of everything that goes on in this house. Why is that?"

Anthony paused, thinking about this. The Cray woman was nosy, that was for sure, but she did seem to know everything that went on. "I actually hadn't thought about that," he said.

"Well, maybe we should. I mean if there's something we need to know, I think we should convince her to tell us," Jeanette said.

"But there's more," Anthony said, watching Jeanette raise her eyebrows in a surprised manner.

"More?" she said.

"I spent a great deal of time down in the basement after you left with the kids. I found some strange paperwork. Some expense reports, a few notes and such. But one letter struck me as odd. It was a formal request by two men named Casale and Elliott in regards to some debt they owed on a piece of property. I think it may be this property."

"Did it specify this property?" Jeanette asked, going into her trial lawyer mode.

"No, but it did mention how the two men would bring out some dirt if they were not given the time they needed to repay the loan."

"Anthony, you're reaching. They could be talking about any property in the country."

"True. But the letter is here. In this house. On *this* property. What if that dirt they threatened to dig up was a clue to what's happened in this house? And possibly what's happened to make that woman so scared." Anthony looked away from his wife. She was piercing him with those eyes, begging him to say something stupid. He knew she wasn't buying any of this. But he had to stay firm.

"What else? Was there anything else down there?" she asked.

"Yes. There was more paperwork. And some old clothes. Oh, and some old Prince albums. I wish we had a record player." Anthony smiled at her, thinking about how young they were when they both heard those Prince albums. Making love in his studio apartment and eating take-out Chinese at three in the morning. Things were so simple then. He went to work, Jeanette went to school. And then they would meet up in the evening and do it all again. That was a great memory.

Jeanette exhaled. She suddenly felt exhausted. The last few days had drained her and now, sitting down here with her husband listening to these stories, she felt simply dead tired. So she exhaled and thought carefully about her words. "I want to talk to the Cray woman. Both of us, together. And then maybe we get some solid answers about this place. And then I want you to come stay with us at the hotel. Away from this place."

"I'll go with you to Harriet's, but then I'm coming home. I miss you and the kids terribly, Jeanette. But I won't leave until this is resolved.'

"Why? What will you gain from all of this? We've been in this house for less than six months. What could you possibly have invested in it?" Jeanette said.

"Something happened here, dammit! Something that will continue to happen unless we find the answers."

"But why you, Anthony? Why do you have to be the fucking great savior? Let someone else move in here and deal with it. It was here before us. Let it go!" Jeanette was standing now, clearly pissed off.

"I'm sorry, Jeanette. But I can't do that. We inherited this problem. And it stops with us. Like it or not, I WILL figure this."

"Even if it costs you your family, Anthony? What happened to you?" She said.

And then there was silence. They both looked anywhere except at each other until Jeanette grabbed her coat from the back of the love seat. She put it on and opened the front door. Anthony watched her, waiting.

"Are we going?" she asked.

"To the Crays?" he said.

"To the Crays."

Anthony grabbed his own coat and walked out the front door.

(21)

Michael was tickling Taylor and she was laughing hysterically. Tears were streaming from her eyes and she was begging for Michael to stop. Lillian Hanover, a friend of Jeanette's from back in college, shouted for the two kids to stop screwing around. Michael stopped tickling Taylor and looked up at Lillian.

"Sorry, gosh," he said.

"Well, can't you hear your sister screaming for mercy? She's gotten the point, Michael," Lillian said.

"Yeah!" Taylor interjected, clearly happy to be done laughing so hard.

"Now, go wash your hands and let's have some lunch. Aunt Lillian made a very special tuna sandwich for you two."

Michael and Taylor both looked at each other and made faces. And then they were both heading towards the bathroom and laughing. Lillian shook her head and set the table for lunch.

When they were well into their sandwiches, and clearly enjoying them, Lillian decided to ask them about the house.

"So what exactly is going on in that house, guys?" she asked.

"What do you mean?" Taylor said in between mouthfuls of her tuna salad sandwich.

"Well, your mom told me that something was going on at home. So I thought I would ask."

"Are we allowed to talk about it?" Michael asked, looking at Taylor for approval.

"Mom didn't say not to," Taylor said.

Both of the kids shrugged their shoulders and kept eating. Lillian just watched them. She could remember when they were born. It seemed like yesterday. Time was like that, she mused. And then she thought of some lesson in college about Einstein's theory regarding time. How it went faster as you got older. If that were true, and it certainly seemed like it was, then she better get cracking on some of her goals because that bad old Father Time was rolling along at a pretty fast clip. And he didn't seem to be slowing down. Lillian smiled, thinking of her time in college with Jeanette. How they partied one night so hard that they both ended up back in their dorm room without any memory of how they got there. They were both fully clothed, thankfully. But it was a horrible feeling nonetheless to know that you got home somehow, but couldn't for the life of you figure out how. Michael burped aloud and Lillian was brought back to the kitchen table, and a story that was about to be told.

"Michael saw something in the kitchen, a lady. She was holding a baby and kept telling my dad to be quiet." Taylor said.

"And who was this woman?" Lillian asked.

"Oh, we don't know. But mom says that she appeared in their bedroom earlier that day."

Michael stopped chewing for a moment and looked at Aunt Lillian. He was searching her face for some reaction. All he found was a small smirk.

"Michael was scared. But I think we were all scared of that woman," Taylor said, looking over to Michael and smiling. He smiled back at her.

"So you think that there's a ghost in your house?" Lillian asked.

"We know there's one. We all saw it," Michael said.

"So why is your Dad still in the house?"

"He thinks he can help the woman."

"Do you think he can help her?" Lillian asked.

"I don't know. I know that mom wants him to get out of that house right away," Michael said.

"And that's why your mom went over there now, right?"

97

"Yes. She said she was coming back with Dad no matter what," Taylor said.

And that was how the conversation ended. They all finished up their lunch and cleaned up the table. Michael and Taylor went outside to play and Aunt Lillian sat at the table doing a Sudoku puzzle. She glanced up occasionally to see if the kids were okay. They were.

(22)

Jeanette pulled on Anthony's arm and held him close as they walked. She put her head against his shoulder, feeling his warmth and wondering why he was so adamant about staying in the house. She could remember a time not too long ago, a time when they were already married for many years when he would be physically ill to be away from her. He would get anxious and run from wherever he was just to get to her. To see her. To kiss her. But now, walking along a lonely stretch of sidewalk somewhere between a home she no longer wanted to be in and the home of a very strange woman, was Jeanette reminded of just how far things had fallen. She pulled on him harder and tried to sink into his jacket. The wind had grown steadily stronger since she arrived this morning and she could feel it's cold fingers swirling around her cheeks. She looked up at Anthony as they walked and smiled. He was a great man, she knew. But now, for whatever reason, he was experiencing something she could not understand. He was going through some strange metamorphosis that involved his children and even his wife. Jeanette didn't pretend she understood. She only walked with the biting wind at her face and a million questions in her mind.

They both stopped at the end of the walkway that lead to the Cray's front door. Anthony looked down at Jeanette and offered up a weak little smile. He pulled her close to him and kissed the top of her head.

"I hope you get the answers you're looking for," he said.

Jeanette didn't answer. She only widened her eyes and sighed. She wasn't even sure this was a good idea. The Cray woman had bothered her from the moment they met in the grocery store. Something was so off about the woman. And now here they were, standing just beyond the threshold, hoping for some sort of truth. Anthony pulled free from her arm and walked up the path.

He pulled on the large brass knocker on the door, banging twice before releasing it. He looked over at his wife, thinking about how beautiful she was. Several seconds passed without an answer. Anthony looked over at Jeanette.

"Try again," she said.

Anthony grabbed the knocker and banged two more times. Several seconds and still nothing.

"Now what?" he asked.

"Now I guess we go home," she said.

They turned to leave, Jeanette once again grabbing his arm and holding him close. Anthony looked back only once, hoping to see Harriet standing in the doorway. But there was nothing. Only the chilly air to guide them as they walked back to their house. It would be a long walk, filled with silence as Jeanette wondered how she could get her husband to leave. But Anthony remained rooted to his cause, even if he had no idea why.

They returned to their own driveway, Jeanette's car sitting quietly near the front porch. She stopped as they got near the front porch. She pulled Anthony towards her and kissed him softly on the mouth. He responded for only a moment before pulling away from her.

"I know you think I'm losing it, Jeanette. But I'm okay."

"Then why won't you leave this place? Why won't you come back to your children?"

"I never left my children. You took them away, remember?" he asked.

"I was concerned for our safety, Anthony. They shouldn't be around this place," Jeanette said.

"I would never let anything happen to my family, dammit! You know that!" Anthony said.

"And what about the things you can't control, Anthony? What about that? Whatever we saw in that house is not anything you can protect us from. Don't you see that? And yet you feel absolutely compelled to stay here, to find answers. Why?"

Anthony swung his fist at the air, angry with himself for losing control yet unable to stop any of it. He wanted to grab Jeanette and shake her, to make her see what he saw. And yet, for the life of him, he could not figure why he wanted to stay. That remained the problem. He had no answers of his own.

"I don't know, Jeanette. I don't know anything."

"Then come stay with us. Get away for a little bit while you sort it out."

"I can't do that. There's something for me to find, some sort of answer that needs discovering. I want to stop the cycle," he said.

Jeanette looked totally perplexed. "What are you talking about? You have no obligations to this place. It's simply wood and brick and stone. Nothing more. And yet you speak like a man with some sort of spiritual connection to this place. We've always been who we are, Anthony. We've always been Jeanette and Anthony and our two kids Michael and Taylor. We've been that way for a long time. We have history together as a family. I have my history growing up. You have your childhood memories. But before that, nothing. Don't you understand? *There is nothing holding you here!*"

Anthony looked shocked. He had never heard his wife scream at him like that. He had never seen her face grow angry and loud words come flying out like daggers. But here she was, hurling at him. He took a moment to internalize everything. He wanted to say something, but no words came out. She was right. He knew she was right. And yet not a single part of him had any intention of leaving. He looked down at the ground and started crying.

They stood silent for several minutes. Jeanette shed some tears of her own, crying into that cold wind. And finally, when she could no longer stand the silence, "You're not coming, are you?" she asked.

Anthony looked up, his face covered with tears. He simply shook his head.

Jeanette turned towards her car and stomped off. She pulled the driver's side door open and looked back at Anthony.

"Fuck you, Anthony," she said, and then got in the car and drove away.

It had grown horribly cold outside.

(23)

Anthony went inside. He turned on the shower and waited for it to heat up. He had an idea about talking to his boss. An idea that maybe the man could shed some light on things. And perhaps he would run across Peter Siegelman in Layout and Design, just so he could punch the smug bastard in the face and take out some of his aggression.

The shower was hot. He stood underneath the flow of water for several minutes, letting the argument with Jeanette wash away. He was angry. Angry with her for cursing at him, but more angry with himself for letting things get to this point so quickly. He could scream. He wanted to see his children more than anything, except getting to the truth about the house. He squirted some cucumber melon shampoo into his hand and smiled at the pleasant odor. He scrubbed his hair, trying his best to get these thoughts out of his head. He scrubbed harder, frothy shampoo falling into his eyes. He wanted to be done with all of this. The whole mess. But not until he knew all there was to know. He rinsed his hair, scrubbed his body with soap, rinsed and then turned the shower off. He stood there, water dripping from his whole body, and let a bit of calm settle in on him. He exhaled deeply and then got out of the shower.

Anthony stood in front of the mirror over the sink looking at the lines around his eyes. He looked so old. But he felt even older, like he had aged twenty years in the past week. He lathered up some shaving cream and shaved, watching the fresh blade strip away a line of shaving cream and the salt and pepper stubble on his face. Each swipe of the blade clearing a path like a clean slate. He vowed to start this day with the knowledge that today would be the last he would be without answers. Little did he know the answers would find him first.

(24)

Anthony peeked into Jonah Castle's office and found it dark. Jonah was not in and his secretary was nowhere in sight. Anthony checked his watch. It was 1:30: a little too late to be out to lunch. But where were they? He looked around the office. He could hear a copier doing its business in an office down the hall and the sound of laughter from someplace else. But Jonah and his secretary were out, that much was obvious. Anthony turned and headed to the elevator.

It was a short ride to the fourth floor where Layout and Design housed its employees. Having missed Jonah, Anthony decided that seeing Peter would make for a lousy substitute, but a substitute nonetheless. The man may be a prick, but he also seemed to be tuned in to what was happening with his house. Anthony cringed, thinking about how badly he wanted to ruin Peter's day. But that wouldn't be conducive to getting answers. So he rounded the corner and was met with a closed office door. Anthony looked at the name on the door: Peter Siegelman, Operations Mgr. Layout and Design. It was the right office, but the man was out. Jonah Castle was out also. Strange. And just when he thought he might be on to something. Anthony pounded his fist against the closed door and headed back towards the elevator.

Behind Anthony, the closed office door of Peter Siegelman cracked open and Harriet Cray peeked through. She watched Anthony get in the elevator and then she stepped from the office.

A moment later, Peter Siegelman and Jonah Castle emerged from the office. The three of them stood in the hallway, watching the elevator doors close. And then they went their separate ways.

(25)

Jeanette pulled into the driveway of her friend Lillian's house. She had barely made it to the front door when her phone rang. She stopped short of the front door and pulled the phone from her purse. It rang again as she flipped it open and answered.

"Hello?" she said.

"Is this Jeanette Morrison?" the voice on the phone asked.

"It is. Who is this?"

"Jeanette, this is Harriet Cray, your neighbor."

A sense of awakening fell over Jeanette, as if a light had gone on in her head and she was suddenly enlightened. "Funny you should call, Harriet. Anthony and I were just at your place, looking to speak with you."

"I would advise you to shut up and listen, Jeanette. What I have to say will be of great interest to you," Harriet said.

The light that had gone on in Jeanette's head had suddenly grown dim and a very sharp chill ripped through her body. Her mother's intuition told her something was wrong. Very wrong. She kept the phone to her ear and made the last few steps to the front door at a rush. She pounded her free fist against the door, hoping to hear anything on the other side. There was only silence.

"They're not there, Jeanette. But they are safe, for the moment."

"What the hell have you done with my children?" Jeanette pounded on the front door again, refusing to believe that her kids were not inside, but no answer came.

"They are with my son and my husband at our home. They are safe. The same cannot be said for your friend, I'm afraid. She put up a terrible fight and had to be dealt with properly."

Jeanette hated the cold tone that Harriet spoke in. She hated how calm and happy she sounded. She wanted to jump through the phone and strangle the woman. Just throttle her until she stopped breathing. And that's when panic settled into Jeanette's chest like a Boa Constrictor and she started to hyperventilate. She dropped the phone on the ground and bent over at the waist, gasping for breath. From the ground, she could hear Harriet's laughter coming from the phone. Jeanette took another moment to catch her breath and then grabbed the phone again. She would need to remain calm. Her kids were the only things that mattered. So for now she would play the game with Harriet Cray.

"Jeanette?" from the phone.

Jeanette picked it up and put it back to her ear. She inhaled deeply, centering herself, the shark on the prowl again.

"Where are my kids?" Jeanette said.

"They are with my son and husband at our home, like I said. They are playing and eating fresh cookies. I promise, they are happy, for the moment."

This last comment prickled Jeanette's skin. *For the moment.* What did that mean? Were they going to be in some sort of danger as the day progressed? Jeanette had no intention of finding out.

"So now what?" she asked.

"So now you come and pick them up. It's that simple." And then the line went dead. Jeanette closed her phone and pounded on the door one more time. She refused to believe that the Cray woman had somehow managed to get her children to come with her and then did something terrible with her best friend, Lillian. When no answer came to the door, Jeanette turned and raced back to her car. She started it up and then pulled out of the driveway. She grabbed the phone from her purse and pulled up Anthony's number.

(26)

Anthony was on his way home when his cell phone rang out on the passenger seat. He looked over and saw that it was Jeanette. He had no desire to talk to her. She had been quite angry with him when they spoke last, and he had no intention of getting cursed at again. Not today, anyway. So he muted the ring tone and continued driving home.

It was an uneventful drive. He thought about everything that had happened to him over the past several months. He thought about how quickly things in his life had changed. And by the time he pulled into his driveway, he was exhausted. He was no closer to getting any answers than when he left the house earlier. So now, all he wanted was to go inside and get drunk. Pull out that special bottle of scotch he kept in his desk up in the library. He wanted to grab a nice cigar from the humidor on the shelf and just smoke and drink until he couldn't see straight. So he got out of the car and headed towards the front door. A strong wind whipped through him and made his coat flutter. Off in the distance, just over the lake, the sun was setting like a huge, orange globe falling away into the horizon. Anthony stopped for a moment and marveled at it. He couldn't remember the last time he looked at a sunset, especially not one so magnificent. And then another gust of chilly wind blew through and he raced up the steps and into the house.

It was cold inside the house, colder than it should have been. From his jacket pocket the cell phone rang again. He pulled it out, checked the ID and saw it was Jeanette again. He looked at the screen, contemplating whether or not he should answer. He let it ring two more times and then flipped it open.

"Hello?" he said. But there was no answer. Jeanette had already hung up. Anthony closed the phone and threw it on the couch. He pulled his jacket off and threw it on top of the phone.

And that's when something moved near the archway to the kitchen. Anthony saw it out of the corner of his eye. He moved towards the kitchen, every muscle in his body tightening up like a coil. He suddenly felt on edge, ready to spring at the first sign of trouble. Another flash of something raced across the kitchen doorway. Anthony paused, feeling intense goose bumps raise up all over his body. And then something giggled in the kitchen. Upstairs, someone screamed. Anthony turned his head quickly towards the stairs and then ran towards them. He took the steps two at a time, bounding up like a lumbering psychotic. He got to the top of the stairs and saw what had made that horrible scream.

The ghostly apparition near the end of the hallway was a boy no older than ten. He was huddled against the corner of the hallway wall, shaking. Anthony could see a black shape materialize, like a snake, and come down hard on the boy's shoulders. The boy screamed out and fresh tears streamed down his face. Anthony winced, feeling like he too had been whipped. And then another shape materialized near the boy. This one was bigger, more like a man. It was hunched over, winding the black whip up for another go at the boy. In the corner, the boy continued to cower.

Anthony knew what he was seeing was just an illusion. It was simply the ghosts of this house, but it didn't make it any easier to watch. The images he was seeing, coupled with the strange events of the past few days, made everything suddenly very clear. The answer seemed painfully obvious. The house wanted someone to watch! And more specifically, it wanted Anthony to watch. It wanted to purge itself of all it had seen, like a bulimic purging after a large meal. So Anthony would oblige, now completely sure of what his purpose in this house was. And yet one small detail bothered him; once he had seen all of the horrors that happened here, would he ever be able to stay here? Or would the slimy decay of death and terrible consequence force him to leave forever? He didn't know. Right now all he could do was watch.

The two ghosts in the corner continued their terrible punishment; the larger man beat the boy mercilessly, laughing as the boy screamed out in pain.

"No more, master!" the little boy screamed, holding his small hands up to shield himself from the next horrible blow. But the man only laughed harder and brought the whip down across the boys face.

Anthony heard something crash in the kitchen. He pulled his gaze away from the boy and went back downstairs. Standing in the doorway of the kitchen was a woman. The same woman holding her baby. The one who looked eerily similar to Maria and Isabella. The woman was holding the baby tight, much like she did on her last visit. Anthony moved forward, arms outstretched towards the woman.

"Let me help you," Anthony said.

The woman stayed put, her eyes watching Anthony like a hawk. He moved closer to her. And then the woman shrieked as another shape moved in front of her. This ghost was a woman. An older woman with a sash over her shoulders and thick gray hair. The woman with the child clutched her baby tighter as the older woman leaned in and grabbed the baby. The two women fought only for a moment and then the baby was free and into the older woman's arms.

"This ain't your baby. It belongs to us now," the older woman said. And then, from the very wall itself came the ghost of a man. The same man who had been beating the boy upstairs. He went to the older woman and grabbed the baby from her arms. Then he turned towards the younger woman and slugged her across the face. She crumpled to the ground.

"This ain't your baby no more, bitch!" the ghostly man said, disappearing back into the wall.

Anthony felt glued to the floor, unable to move yet completely certain that he could help. But he also knew better. What he was seeing was in the past. None of it could be changed. The house continued to purge. And Anthony continued to watch.

Outside, the wind had grown ferocious.

(27)

Jeanette was driving too fast. She knew it was dangerous, but right now her children were all that mattered. She drove past their house, noticing Anthony's car parked out front. Why didn't he answer his phone? Was something wrong? Was he hurt? A million thoughts raced through her mind as she zipped by and came upon the Cray house. She pulled into the driveway by way of the front lawn, ripping up a huge patch of grass in the process. But Jeanette could have cared less. Her children.

She slammed the car into park and left the engine running. In a moment she was out the door and racing up the sidewalk to the front door. It opened just as she was about to knock. Harriet stood in the doorway, smiling.

"So nice of you to come," Harriet said.

"Where are . . ." Jeanette started, but immediately Michael and Taylor came running up behind Harriet. They pushed their way past her and hugged Jeanette.

"Oh, Mom. How are you?" Taylor asked.

"I'm great!" Jeanette said, fighting back the urge to cry. She looked up at Harriet and gave her a sharp glance. The woman only smiled back.

"So where's Aunt Lillian?" Jeanette asked the kids, making sure to look up only briefly to gauge Harriet's reaction to the question.

"She left," Michael said.

Jeanette continued to look up at Harriet. "She left?"

Harriet smiled even wider, exposing too many teeth that were far too perfect to be real. "She did indeed," Harriet said.

Jeanette bristled under her skin. She wanted to grab this woman by the hair and pull her to the ground. Instead, she ushered the kids towards the car. "Get in the car and warm up. I just want to talk to Mrs. Cray here for a minute."

Taylor and Michael looked back only briefly and then raced towards the car. They got inside and shut the door.

Jeanette turned her full attention back to Harriet.

"Let me make this real clear," Jeanette started. "If you ever touch my children again I will kill you. Is that understood?"

"Oh, I understand, Mrs. Morrison. The question is, how much of this do *you* understand?"

Jeanette tilted her head in a curious manner. "What are you talking about?"

"You so desperately want answers but you're afraid to just look," Harriet said.

Jeanette was growing frustrated with these riddles. She felt like Harriet was intentionally talking in circles. She wanted to scream.

"Why did you tell me on the phone that my friend Lillian was dead?" Jeanette asked.

"I never said she was dead, Mrs. Morrison. I simply said she had to be dealt with. I'm afraid she's had a terrible accident on her way home, though. A terrible accident."

Jeanette raised her hand, wanting nothing more than to strike Harriet down right where she stood. But she knew better. She knew her kids were watching from the car. So she put her hand down and simply glared at Harriet Cray. A smell like rotten fruit wafted out from the open front door and Jeanette frowned.

"I'm thrilled that we finally got a chance to talk, you and I. I've always had the utmost respect for you and your husband. And your children are simply precious," Harriet said.

Jeanette continued to glare, knowing that this woman was trying her hardest to get a rise out of her. She had seen it a thousand times before when she was in court, arguing a case before a jury and some arrogant attorney was working her. In the case of the courtroom, it was simply because she was a woman. No self-respecting attorney worth his salt could let a woman beat him in court. Assholes. They learned the hard way, unfortunately. And now, listening to Harriet spout off at the mouth, did Jeanette feel just like she was back in court, getting throttled by some prickly defense attorney. And a sudden thrill rushed over her. The blood in the water attracting the shark.

"Are you finished?" Jeanette asked.

"It depends. For the day? Yes. But you and I will see each other again. We always have," Harriet said.

But Jeanette had already turned her back and was walking away towards the car. She never heard Harriet's last comment.

(28)

Anthony followed the noise down into the basement. He took the stairs slowly, watching each step as if it might disappear under his feet. A strange glow emanated from down below. Anthony knew there were ghosts down there, but he didn't care. He wanted to see this thing through. He knew if he could only let the house finish whatever it might be trying to tell him, then he could finally be with his family again. So he continued down into the odd glow of the basement, feeling completely certain for the first time in months.

Just beyond the bottom of the stairs the ghostly image of the little boy reappeared. He looked happy this time, running around a small ball near his feet. Anthony could hear other children laughing with the little boy. And then suddenly, a whole group of children appeared, ghostly and translucent, but very much there. Anthony stood where he was, at the base of the stairs, and simply watched. After all, it was the only thing he could do.

"Pass it!" the little boy said to some other child. There was a quick rush of giggles and then one of the kids screamed.

"He's coming," one of them said.

"C'mon, follow me," another shouted.

The children rallied behind a stack of boxes and did their best to hide. From the top of the stairs another shape appeared. Anthony had seen this one before. It was the man who was beating the little boy; the same man who took the baby from the old woman. Anthony knew the children were very afraid of this man.

The large ghost rambled down the stairs and passed by Anthony, leaving a cold gust of air in its wake. He paused, looked around the basement, and then lumbered towards the boxes where the kids were hiding. Anthony could see the children cowering, clearly afraid of the larger ghost. He could only imagine what type of horror these children were exposed to. What type of torture they might be subject to. Anthony had to keep reminding himself that none of this was happening anymore. It was all in the past. A horrible manifestation that simply would not leave until it was able to share it's dark secret with someone. And right now, the only person who decided to stick around was Anthony Morrison. And what he was about to see would scar him forever.

Upstairs, Jeanette had come through the front door . . .

(29)

. . . and saw her living room filled with ghostly apparitions. There were women doing chores in the living room. On the couch she saw an older man kissing a black woman on the neck. The woman looked uncomfortable and sad. Jeanette thought she saw tears in the woman's eyes. To her left, from the kitchen, Jeanette could hear the sound of pots clanging. She could the rustle of many voices.

"Anthony!" she called out. She knew he was here, but she also knew something was very wrong. The place had an odd sort of electricity running through it. The walls seemed too far away and the air seemed to sing with an array of inhuman voices. Jeanette moved towards the kitchen, and ultimately, towards the doorway to the basement. She saw the door standing open and her husband standing at the bottom of the steps, looking frightened.

"Anthony," she said, much softer than she expected, and was actually shocked to see him look up at her.

"Don't come down here," he said. Jeanette could see a terrible sadness in his eyes.

"Anthony, what is it?" she asked.

"Where are the kids?" he asked from the dark well of the stairs.

"They're in the car, sweetie. Are you okay?"

Anthony looked towards whatever was in the basement and then up at his wife. "It's horrible down here," he said.

"I'm coming down," she said, taking the first step on the stairs. The sound of glass shattering from the kitchen startled her and she nearly lost her balance. It sounded like a window crashing in. And as if to confirm her thoughts, Jeanette felt a strong gust of wind come rushing past her, down into the basement. She could feel how terribly cold it was. Below her, Anthony shivered.

"Please, Jeanette. Don't come down here," Anthony said.

Jeanette took another step. Another crash from the kitchen, this time the sound of pots and pans crashing to the ground. Jeanette looked back and saw someone race past the doorway. It looked like a child. Moments later another shape rushed past. This time it was a larger man with something in his hands. A second later Jeanette heard the terrible scream of a child. She shivered herself, but turned her attention back to Anthony, and making it to the bottom of the stairs.

"Jeanette, please!" Anthony said, tears streaming down his face now.

"I'm coming own there, so just shut up!" she said.

She took two more steps and another loud noise from somewhere above her. She knew terrible things were happening in the house. She didn't dare to think about what those things might be. Whatever was at the bottom of the stairs would probably be enough. Whatever was making her husband cry had to be terrible indeed. She took the rest of the stairs at a run and stopped dead in her tracks at the bottom. She knew now why Anthony didn't want her coming down here. She also knew with absolute certainty that she would never be able to un-see what was in front of her. It was burned into her mind like the image of a bright light when you close your eyes. Except that this image would never go away.

Anthony grabbed her and held her tight against him. And together they cried.

They made their way up the stairs together, Anthony holding Jeanette tight in his arms, keeping her face against his chest as they walked. He didn't want her to have to see anything else. What they saw in the basement was more than enough. Anthony only hoped it was enough to let the spirits here rest in peace. He wanted nothing more than for those children who suffered in this house to be able to rest. As it stood now, they were reliving these horrors over and over again. And now, maybe, they could finally smile for eternity.

They made it to the top of the stairs and Anthony closed the door behind them. Jeanette pulled free. Together they looked around the kitchen and assessed the damage. Every cabinet had been pulled open and all of the contents were spilled across the floor. Two windows in the kitchen had indeed shattered and glass was everywhere. The kitchen door that led to the backyard was banging against the wall in a steady rhythmic thump. But no ghosts ran free in here. It seemed quiet. In fact, the whole house seemed quiet.

Anthony looked back into the living room and saw nothing but his own furniture. There were no ghosts or lingering spirits that he could see. Jeanette brushed past him and raced up the stairs.

"Jeanette, wait!" Anthony said. And then he was off, chasing her up the stairs.

They met in their bedroom. Jeanette was standing near the bed and looking out the window that looked out onto the lake. Anthony came up behind her and put his hands on her shoulders. She put one of her own hands on his.

"Is it over?" she asked.

Anthony paused, thinking hard about the answer. He didn't truly know if it was over. But it *felt* over. Something felt different in here, like a great weight had been lifted.

"I hope so," he said.

And then Jeanette looked to her right and down at their bed. She remembered that morning not long ago when she saw her husband on top of another woman. She remembered how she felt. She also remembered that what she saw on the bed was not really her husband. It was a ghost like all the rest. But another thought also peeked through. And this one bothered her. If what they saw in the house in the last fifteen minutes was something that had happened in the past, then what was to say that what she saw that morning was not also something that happened in the past; that her husband had really been with another woman in this house? She closed her eyes and frowned. Behind her, Anthony leaned in and kissed her neck.

And that's when she knew that it didn't really matter now. She was suddenly the happiest she had been in a long time. Jeanette turned around and kissed Anthony on the mouth. He kissed her back.

(Epilogue)

Anthony clipped another rose from the bush and handed it to Michael. He took it with his small, gloved hands and bundled it with the others.

"When are mom and Taylor coming back?" he asked.

"I'm not sure, but I would imagine when they finish up at the store," Anthony said.

Michael layered his bundle of roses on the ground and pulled his gloves off. He stood up. "Dad?"

Anthony looked up at him from where he was kneeling. "Yes?" he said.

"What kind of things happened in this house?"

"Well, there was a time not too long ago, son, when people in this country did not treat each other very nice." Anthony was weighing his words very carefully. He knew he would one day have to fill his son in on why black folks were sometimes treated differently, but also how far they had come. Life's atrocities sometimes took a backseat to the good stuff. And right now, Anthony did not want to share the atrocities with his son. He wanted him to remember the good stuff. "And unfortunately, some of that bad stuff happened here in this house."

"Is that why we're leaving?" Michael asked.

"Yes it is," Anthony said.

"Are you sad about that?" Michael said.

Anthony thought long and hard about that question. He was sad, but not as sad as he thought he should be. Something tragic had happened here and he was a part of that. But he also knew now that his family was the only thing that mattered. He thought back to those long nights when he was alone in the house, contemplating his life and feeling so empty. That seemed like such a long time ago. And then Richard LeBrock's Brigadier general horn sounded from the front of the house and Anthony was startled from his thoughts.

"Mr. LeBrock's here, Michael. Let's go greet him," Anthony said. They both made their way to the front of the house.

Richard was waiting for them, holding a stack of papers in his hands. "Hello, gentlemen," Richard said.

Anthony shook his hand and took the paperwork. "I'm really sorry about all of this, Richard," Anthony said.

"You have nothing to be sorry about. I'm just going to have a hell of a time trying to get rid of this place. I'm not really sure what's happened here, though. And since you're not talking too much," Richard broke off and laughed. Anthony and Michael laughed with him. Richard got in his truck and drove away, the brake lights flickering only once as he sped off past the copse of trees that shielded the house from any sort of civilization.

Anthony watched him drive away and then turned to Michael. The boy was still, looking off at the house.

"Why don't you go out back and make sure that you have all your stuff together. Mom and Taylor are going to be back any minute now," Anthony said.

Michael seemed to snap out of his gaze just then and he turned to look up at his Dad. "Okay," he said and trotted off towards the back of the house.

"I love you," Anthony called out after him. He was not sure why he said it just then, but it would be the last words he ever spoke to his son. It would be the last time he ever saw him.

From the *Cleveland Plain-Dealer*, dated March 21, 2009.

SCRANTON- *The search continues for the missing Morrison boy, gone since March 7. Police still have very little to go on besides several anonymous tips. "This is something that happens when anyone goes missing." Police Chief Prince told us. "It's all about weeding out the kooks from the serious information. But we will not give up our search for the boy. Whether he's alive or dead, we will find him." The boy was found missing from his home on Mercy Street on the very day that the Morrison family was moving out. No suspects have been made public and the Morrison family has refused to comment.*

From an article in *Time* magazine titled 'Horror and Fairy Tales' by contributing writer Tony Castle, dated June 7, 2009.

'They said the house smelled of apples. It was a startling contrast to an otherwise horrifying scene. The two detectives, Sgt. Mark Peterson and Stan Grossman, who broke the case talked about how much carnage was in the house. One of them even cited Hansel and Gretel when talking about what they found. So how does a mystery that spans nearly two hundred years only now get exposed? That was the question that Time magazine put to these two men in our exclusive interview.'

What follows is an excerpt from that interview.

'What we found in the house defied description. Never in all our years on the force had we seen or even heard about such things. And the only thought that kept coming back into my head was that fairy tale, Hansel and Gretel.'
'Can you explain further?'
'Yeah, it was like that story where that witch was luring the kids into her home and then cooking them. It was awful. But what really strikes me is how long this whole ordeal went on. We're talking nearly two hundred years of murders being committed

right in suburbia. Several generations of this family doing what they do and getting away with it.'

At this point we had to stop because both Mark Peterson and Stan Grossman began to cry. I resumed my interview the following day but was asked to keep it informal and off the record. What I learned was both shocking and repulsive. It was a lesson in the possibilities of evil in every one of us. I only wish that so many children did not have to suffer. I was, however, allowed to print the following quote from the father of the last victim.

'Had I known then what was happening next door to my house, in the Cray house, I would have done something about it. And now, looking back, I guess I always knew something was wrong anyway. I only wish I could have my son back. But she took him from me and I will never forgive her for that. I will never be okay with that.'

As a parent I guess I can understand.

On May 16th, 2009 a team of twelve officers, led by Detectives Peterson and Grossman, forcefully entered the home of Harriet and Jonah Cray. They found the remains of several thousand corpses buried in the backyard and throughout the house. The Cray's had a son, Peter, who was also arrested for his part in the atrocities. The entire family was finally brought to justice before a jury. They were all sentenced to three consecutive life sentences without chance of parole.

Peter hanged himself in his first night in prison. Jonah, charged as the leader of all of the murders, ripped his own throat out and bled to death in his cell. Harriet Cray is still alive and serving her sentences.

(One Last Question)

"There's just a few things I need to know, Anthony," Jeanette said.

"Okay," he replied, closing the door to Taylor's bedroom and walking softly towards the living room with Jeanette on his arm. They both plopped down on the couch and snuggled up to each other.

"So much of what has happened seems like a dream to me. Some of it I'm not even sure was real at all. Do you feel like that?" she asked.

Anthony thought long and hard about the question. He did feel that way sometimes, but mostly it was because he was still struggling with the death of his son.

"I do. But I also know that what we saw, and what we experienced was traumatic. I just wish I could have seen all of it coming."

"What do you mean?" Jeanette said.

"Well, mostly the stuff with my boss. I mean how did I not know that him and Peter were part of the family. It's maddening!" he said.

"No one knew, sweetie. I mean it was a lie that they lived for a very long time. And you were not the only one who was surprised."

"I guess you're right, but there's just so many other things," he said.

"Like what?"

"Well, for starters, all of that shit I found in the basement. It all seemed so relevant,"

"Relevant to whom? To you? That stuff was there when we moved in and it's probably still there right now. It was only relevant because you wanted it to be relevant. If you tried hard enough-and you did, by the way-you could have made a connection with anything. You wanted so desperately to find answers, Anthony." Jeanette paused here and bit her lip. She wanted so badly to blame her husband for everything. She wanted to slap him and tell him what a fool he was for letting them move into that house. But she didn't. She didn't because she also knew that it was not his fault at all. Things sometimes happened. And in this case it was something very bad. But it was not her husband's fault. So she leaned in and kissed him instead. It was a soft kiss, on his temple.

Jeanette got up from the couch and went into the kitchen. She pulled two Heineken's from the fridge and grabbed a bottle opener from the drawer. She popped the beers open and then made her way back towards the living room, pausing in the doorway. She tilted her head and wrinkled her brow. She had one more question for Anthony. Just one more thing that was eating at her; one last itch to scratch.

Anthony looked up at his wife from the couch. "What's wrong?" he asked.

"There's just one more thing I have to know. It's driving me crazy. And after all that we've been through, I think I deserve an honest answer."

"Okay," Anthony said.

Jeanette came into the room and handed Anthony a beer. She took a big swallow from hers and then wiped her lips with her forearm.

"Have you ever cheated on me?" she asked.

END

Printed in the United States
141170LV00007B/2/P

9 781440 129315